D0660907

CLOUD OF WITNESSES

Cloud
of
Witnesses

Jane Hertenstein

Golden Alley Press
Emmaus, Pennsylvania

This book is a work of fiction. Although references to real people, places, and events are used to create authenticity, the story, characters, and dialog are all products of the author's imagination.

© 2018 Jane Hertenstein

All rights reserved. No part of this publication may be reproduced without the prior written permission of the publisher, except in the case of brief quotations embodied in critical reviews and certain other noncommercial uses permitted by copyright law. For permission requests, contact the publisher at the address below.

Golden Alley Press
37 S. Sixth Street
Emmaus, Pennsylvania 18049

www.goldenalleypress.com

The text of this book is set in Adobe Caslon
Book design by Michael Sayre

Printed in the United States of America

Publisher's Cataloging-in-Publication Data

Names: Hertenstein, Jane, 1958- author.
Title: Cloud of witnesses / Jane Hertenstein.
Description: Emmaus, PA : Golden Alley Press, 2018. | Grades 5-8.
Identifiers: LCCN 2018946515 | ISBN 978-1-7320276-2-6 (pbk.) | ISBN 978-1-7320276-3-3 (ebook)
Subjects: LCSH: Children's stories. | CYAC: Nineteen seventies--Fiction. | Appalachian Region--Fiction. | Friendship--Fiction. | Coming of age--Fiction. | Loyalty--Fiction. | BISAC: JUVENILE FICTION / Historical / United States / 20th Century. | JUVE-NILE FICTION / Social Themes / Adolescence. | JUVENILE FICTION / Social Themes / Friendship. | JUVENILE FICTION / School & Education.
Classification: LCC PZ7.H432435 Clo (print) | LCC PZ7.H432435 (ebook) | DDC [Fic]--dc23.

Front cover photograph: © *Nathan Cameron*
Front cover art: © *Nathan Cameron*
Back cover photograph of the author: © *Elena Börner*

10 9 8 7 6 5 4 3 2 1

RO454186844

To Esther Hershenhorn for her continual cheerfulness and encouragement

A Stranger in the Foothills

I leaned over the sink to see what exactly was wrong with my teeth. The mirror reflected what I already knew—they were a little crooked, slouchy as if too lazy to stand up straight. Thankfully, they weren't as bad as my brother's teeth. Larry's mouth reminded me of a dark alley with twists and turns. I heaped my brush with a mound of toothpaste and began to scrub. Back and forth, up and down—until Granny banged on the door and demanded her time.

Old trailers such as ours tend to shift and everything gets off-kilter. The bathroom door slipped and opened an inch or two to reveal me foaming at the mouth like a rabid animal.

"Roland!" she screamed. "Quit using up all the toothpaste."

I quickly cupped my hand under the faucet, swished, and washed off my bubble-beard.

"What's it matter to you, you don't have any teeth," I said with a little too much sass.

She shot me a look that was all knives. I surrendered the bathroom.

"Now, Roland," Mama started up from the kitchen where she was fixing me a "good" breakfast, being that it was my first day of school. "You know Granny's got those two little ones in the front. She's just missing her chewers."

I searched through the pile of clothes by the bunk bed Daddy had made for me with plywood he had taken out of an old house. Where was my new T-shirt? The only really white one I owned since most of the others were grey or permanently sweat-stained at the armpits.

"Mama," I wailed. "I can't find my shirt."

"I washed it," she called back. "It's out on the line."

I rushed outside to find it damp, practically dripping. I put it on anyway. The school bus was set to arrive in only five minutes.

"That shirt's all wet," Mama said, as I sat down.

Granny was out of the bathroom and at her place at the table. "That's how you get polio."

"Kids don't get polio anymore," I told her. "There's a shot for that."

Granny stared down her bumpy nose at me and then puked up a little bit in a coffee can at her feet.

Granny used to have terrible ulcers until doctors operated on her about a year ago and took out part of her stomach. Because she wasn't able to digest large portions all at once, she kept a coffee can by her chair in case she had to quick lighten the pressure of a full stomach.

Mama's idea of a good breakfast was a plate of runny scrambled eggs. We used bacon grease for everything and there was a little bit of congealed fat mixed in with the egg soup. I contemplated siphoning the whole mess off into Granny's coffee can.

"Ain't that your bus?" Mama observed from the kitchen window where she stood at the stove stirring up mush for Granny.

"Shoot!" I jumped up and knocked over Granny's coffee can. "Hey!" she yelled as I ran out the door.

The bus was already down the hill and up half of another.

Mama came out and stood with me in the dust-cloud left in its wake. "We can get Larry up to take ya, baby."

Larry was still in the rack, in the top bunk.

"No," I said a little too quickly. "I can ride and get there in time."

I fetched my bike out from underneath the trailer and brushed the cobwebs and grit that had accumulated from the past few days off the seat and handlebars. I took off, my book bag bouncing up and down on my back.

Not only was my shirt wet from the dew, but I was also working up a hearty sweat. Road silt churned up by the bus drifted onto my shirt and skin. My white T-shirt was no longer white.

A grasshopper suddenly jumped and thudded me in the forehead. I stopped cold and rubbed the spot. My hand was wet where the grasshopper had peed a little. I got back on my bike and double-pedaled.

By the time I arrived at Athens Middle School I looked like mud man. My hair, so carefully combed that morning, was dust-coated a shade lighter than its usual brown, the color of Daddy's tobacco from which he rolled his own. Kids dressed in brand new back-to-school outfits passed me on the covered walkways. Straight away I knew: I was all wrong.

At the end of seventh grade I had taken a test. Not a spelling test (I was a whiz at spelling), not a math test (I got all A's in math), not a test on who won what war when (I did alright in history), and not one of those true-false, multiple-choice science tests (you'd have to be a pretty bad guesser not to get at least eighty percent right), but a "comprehensive" test that did it all at once. I was given long paragraphs to read and then answered some questions. Afterwards Daddy came in with me for a special parent-child conference. The principal at Stuart Elementary, the county school I'd been attending since kindergarten, sat across a desk from us. "Mr. Tanner, your son has tested high."

Daddy's eyebrows shot up. I could tell he thought that meant I was on drugs.

The principal said, "We would like to place Roland in a special program for gifted children."

At that, Daddy turned all red and looked down at his hands folded stiffly in his lap, his fingertips stained from the unfiltered cigarettes he smoked. "This ain't welfare, is it?" he had to ask.

The principal told him no and after that Daddy relaxed.

Later Mama and Daddy got a letter in the mail telling them that I would need to be bused down into town, to Athens Middle School.

I found my homeroom just in time to take a seat. A quick pit check made me wish I had some cologne or something to mask the smell. The teacher began by taking roll call.

Behind me I heard an exaggerated sniffing. "Anyone smell skunk?" came a deep voice. I turned around, wondering why a man was in our classroom. A kid in a green and white Ohio Bobcats jersey with a buzz cut gave me the stink eye. I quick turned back around.

The homeroom teacher, who had bushy red hair and a face like a squirrel, continued reading off names. "Kyle Messerhoff?" The man-kid behind me called out, "Here."

A girl with honey-blonde hair sat next to me. The way she wore her hair reminded me of Farrah Fawcett from a poster Larry had taped to the wall beside his bunk bed. "Patty Topinski," the teacher called out and the girl raised her hand. She smiled at me, her teeth lining up evenly like white-washed pickets in a fence row.

"Hussein Reza." The squirrelly teacher stumbled over the syllables.

To my left a dark-haired boy shyly raised his hand. Nearly as skinny as Larry, he looked to be all elbows and sharp angles.

"That is an unusual name. Where are you from,

Hussein?"

"*Hassan*," he stressed. "I'm from—my family I mean—we're from Iran."

"Iran!" She pounced on the word, only she pronounced it as I-ran. "That's over in the Middle East, isn't it?"

"He's gonna wish he ran," Kyle "whispered" loud enough for the room to hear. A couple of kids snickered.

"Kyle, please," said Miss Squirrel in a frowning tone, though she was actually smiling. "Be nice." She turned back to Hassan. "What brings you to Athens?"

"My father is visiting faculty at the university. He works in the Accelerator Lab." I noticed he didn't talk like me, or anybody I knew in Ohio.

"Well, that sounds interesting." Miss Squirrel was ready to go on.

When people say interesting, I'd learned they usually aren't that interested. It was like saying nice and not meaning it at all. She read off my name. "Roland Tanner."

Except she said Row-land, as if it were two names.

Like a fool I tried to correct her, saying it like my family has always done, drawing it out like a banner unfurled. "It's *Rahl-end*."

She smiled. "Interesting." I lowered my head as if

studying my hands clenched in front of me.

Behind me, in his "whisper," I heard Kyle. "Trailer trash."

We were the worst kind of people. Not like the townies, folks who lived in houses that lined the streets, and not like the hippies, who smoked weed and lived communally on the edge of town. Not like the students whose parents worked for the university or were professor's kids. Truth be told, my dad was "between" jobs, meaning he was out of work.

After roll call she quickly excused us to rotate to our next class. On the way out the door Kyle hip-checked me into the door frame. In the center of his freckled forehead was a pimple about the size of a boiled peanut. "Oh, sorry." He tried to make it look like an accident.

"S'kay." I just shook it off and shifted my new Trapper-Keeper notebook under my arm. It was important, I told myself, to not do anything stupid.

My very first gifted class was English, which gave me a boost of confidence, since at Stuart I had been an A-1 reader. Always in the elementary grades I was getting citations for the many books I read.

No one in my family liked to read. Every once in a while I'd look up from a book to find Daddy staring at me as if I were a strange bug that had crawled in from outside. He'd turn away quick as if he'd been caught. Reading made it only more obvious that I was different, and the more I read the more I felt like a stranger amongst my own kin.

Ms. Knudsen handed out brand new copies of a paperback book.

At my old school all the textbooks had been old and worn. Once I had been assigned a spelling book that had Larry's name on the inside cover. I flipped through it and saw that he'd drawn googly-eyed, big-bosomed monsters and turned most of the U's into O's. And my desktop had been grooved with the initials of the last ten students who'd sat there and the initials of everyone they'd ever had a crush on. When writing with a ballpoint pen, I had had to be careful not to poke through my notebook paper. My pen glided without hitting speed bumps as I wrote my name on the inside cover.

Ms. Knudsen said we would be starting a unit on mythology. The cover illustration on my new book was of a man with a human torso, but with the legs and butt of a goat.

I let my mind wander as Ms. Knudsen went over the introduction. "You'll see some of this same material if you're selected for *Whiz Kidz*."

Whiz Kidz was a Saturday afternoon TV show broadcast out of Columbus. It was a contest of wit and academic strength between students from different schools. I'd seen it maybe two times when changing channels. It seemed extremely boring and cheesy.

Though it was September it still felt like August. It was maybe a hundred degrees in the classroom. Kids fanned themselves with the book. I looked over at Patty. I could just imagine her in a red swimsuit, the kind Farrah Fawcett wore in Larry's poster. She seemed a sweet, sweet siren. Hassan appeared all storm-tossed and lost, while Kyle reminded me of Cyclops with that big, red, swollen zit in the middle of his forehead.

Suddenly I became aware of Ms. Knudsen pausing by my desk. "Perhaps you can share with the class your thoughts on mythology, Roland," she said.

I sat up straighter. "Uh . . . uh, ma'am."

Kyle snickered. I licked my lips and swallowed hard. I was surrounded by town kids, staring at me in my stained clothes and scruffy sneakers. "I know these gods got special powers and all," I ventured, "but if a person just uses his brain he can usually outwit his enemies. You know, put their eye out."

Ms. Knudsen turned to the blackboard. "Good observation, Roland."

Piercing the Eye

Lunch in the cafeteria was again whole new territory. At Stuart everyone was eligible for the hot lunch. Here, students brought their lunches from home and ate sandwiches with thick slices of lunch meat.

One look at the serving line and I understood why kids packed a lunch. The green beans were Three-Mile Island green, radiating a nuclear neon, and the cooked carrots looked like they'd been injected with cancer-causing red dye #5. The steam-table hot dogs were the same color as the mold growing inside the shower stall at home.

But I was hungry—especially after skipping Mama's "good" breakfast. So after grabbing a carton of chocolate milk and the bread option I began to look for a place to sit.

Deciding where and *who* to sit with could determine my entire middle school fate. I looked over the cafeteria. Clusters of kids, laughing and talking with their mouths full, hogged most of the tables. The safest thing for me was to sit by myself. I found a seat at a table off in a corner.

"Whoa, buddy, what do you call that?" Kyle plopped down beside me, straddling the bench-seat. Above his lip was the smudge of a mustache. His lardy face reminded me of a block of government American cheese, the kind passed out at the Salvation Army.

"What?" I asked.

"That trash you're eating." He guffawed. "Get it, trailer *trash*."

This guy was as annoying as Granny, but I'd learned to ignore her. So I just kept chewing my buttered bread.

After a minute, he started up again. "Check it out."

He pointed his sandwich toward Hassan, who was scanning the lunchroom for a place to sit. If according to the middle school pecking order the foreign kid was at the bottom, then I'd gladly move up a notch. Hassan took a seat at the end of the table.

I busied myself trying to force open the stubborn cardboard spout of my milk carton.

"Hi guys!" Patty pulled up on the other side of me. As she sat down I caught the scent of lilacs and Irish Spring soap. She was the nicest girl I'd ever smelled. Not that I'd smelled that many. Anyway, I was afraid to look at her, afraid of all the backward things I might do or say.

"Roland," she addressed me. "You transferred in, didn't you?"

I nodded.

"From the county school." Kyle made county sound like a dirty word. Like cootie and county was the same thing.

Patty kept up her questioning. "Do you live near Dow Lake?"

But before I could answer, she went on. "I love that place. I love to roll down the hill by the dam. Have you ever done that?"

Again, she didn't give me time to answer.

"Or do you live near Stroud's Run?" she asked.

Stroud's Run was the state park down the road from where I lived.

"I once saw a coyote in the parking lot there," she added.

"I see coyotes all the time. Hear them in the woods at night." I finally got a chance to talk.

"Cool!"

I was beginning to loosen up and feel comfortable with the fact she was sitting next to me. "My dad shoots them."

Her face went still. Kyle suddenly seemed interested. "With a gun?"

I changed the subject. "What's he eating?"

Hassan was chomping on a crackery-kind of bread with a filling that looked like mashed wood chips.

"Do they even use knives and forks in Iran?" Kyle mused out loud.

"Shush," Patty tried to hush me. "He can hear you."

"Or do they scoop food with their fingers?" Kyle gave me a friendly punch in the side that smarted and made me wince.

Hassan stood. I thought he was going to leave the cafeteria. Instead he walked over to us. "Just so you know Iran is the cradle of civilization. It is where man learned to cultivate crops, domesticate animals. It is the birthplace of many religions. You seem to know nothing."

The zit on Kyle's forehead pulsed. "Just to set the record straight, I know about the Cradle of Civilization and all that stuff. And maybe you'll find that out when I'm picked for *Whiz Kidz* and you and this joker here—"

Me?

"Are on the sidelines, watching."

Hassan didn't seem fazed. "I'm not worried. For I plan to try out for the Academic Bowl or *Whiz Kidz* as you call it. Perhaps you should be the one to watch out."

Where was a lunchroom monitor when you needed one? I thought they were going to start sparring over who invented iron tools first. Hassan turned and tossed his lunch in the garbage and left.

"Whoa—" I started, but was interrupted by Patty.

"I'm ashamed of you boys."

"God, you sound like a teacher or something," Kyle complained.

Patty froze him with an icy stare.

He wadded up his lunch sack and sank a bank shot from about seven feet back. As he got up he bumped me in the back of the head just as I was taking a sip of milk, spilling chocolate milk down my already wrecked shirt. "See ya later, moron."

Patty quickly gathered up her books and lunch box. Muttering, "Coyote killer," she left in a huff.

I was back to where I had started: alone. Like a true mortal, I'd only managed to poke myself in the eye.

The Arrowhead

Larry's rusted-red Chevy Impala came barreling toward me just as I was about to steer my bike off the blacktop and onto our rutted gravel road. He was driving hell-bound right down the raised-crown center of the road. He ground to a halt, spraying pea-size scree.

"Whew! You look like something the cat drug in."

"Thanks a lot, Larry." I stopped pedaling.

"Need a ride, little buddy?" He had to yell over his blaring eight-track. "Throw your bike in the trunk and get in."

I undid the rope holding the trunk down and set the bike in before retying the knot.

As soon as I got situated, Larry started up. "Granny's in one of her moods. Tearing up the whole house, she is."

When the doctors opened her up last year to have a look they said it was like she'd drank battery acid all her life. They couldn't repair the lining of her stomach; it was so corroded and full of holes. So what they did was make a little pouch out of what was left. Ever since then she'd had pain, howling pain where she'd sit up at night screaming so that no one slept. The only thing that helped, that calmed her right down, was her painkillers. When they kicked in Granny was a Christian. Before long, though, the codeine wore off and she went back to cussing and hollering to beat the devil. One minute Granny could be sweet as an angel, singing old hymns and praising Jesus, and then the next minute giving me hell. I had a feeling her one minute of goodness for today had already come and gone.

Larry burned rubber as he pulled out, one hand on the steering wheel while the other hand popped the ring-top on a cold beer he kept in a small cooler between his feet. Larry always drove like a maniac. He acted like he owned the whole road, driving whatever speed he wanted, ignoring all the signs, and pretty much wreaking havoc and wrecking fenders wherever he went.

"Guess what?"

"What?" I shouted and reached over and turned down the Doobie Brothers.

"I got me a job." He acted like he'd done something no one else had ever attempted.

"That's great, Larry. Watch it now, ya almost nicked that cat scamperin' across the road." I hung onto the door, which tended to fling open when the car went around corners. Larry had bungee-corded it, but there was still a two- or three-inch gap.

"Damn! I was aimin' to hit it."

He took a long sip. "At the Athens Fall Festival, operatin' the Tilt-A-Hurl."

"I think that ride's called the Tilt-A-Whirl, Larry."

"Not with me running it, it ain't. I'm gonna have all those little kids hurling, crying out for their mamas, I am." Larry rounded a corner at about ninety miles an hour. As the bungee cord stretched thin, I gripped my seat, hoping not to fall out. In a second it snapped back with a thump.

Larry looked straight at me. "I'm getting out of here, boy. After the carnival leaves town they're traveling all over southeastern Ohio, then heading down to Kentucky and Tennessee, and eventually to Florida where they winter before starting up again in the spring. This here's my big chance to make some money and see the world."

Barely looking at the road, he swerved to avoid a mailbox and ran up into someone's lawn. A lady came out and yelled at us as he backed up over her flowers and tore up the grass.

I wished I was the one leaving. I feared if I didn't get off the ridge someday, I'd be killed either by Larry's so-called driving or one of Granny's sour moods. I closed my eyes and prayed for someday soon.

We pulled up into the front yard.

The lot our trailer sat on was littered with car parts and the frames of five or six cars up on cement blocks that Larry was working on or had worked on and would never move again. Down in the ravine behind the trailer, but not completely hidden from sight, was a junk pile of rusted tin cans, an old bed frame, and the carcass of a washing machine Larry had tried to fix. He got it to spin at about a hundred miles an hour until it shredded the clothes inside the drum. Anything that didn't work or that Larry had messed with usually ended up down the hill in the junk pile.

Granny hobbled out of the trailer and pointed her four-legged cane at me. "What in the world happened to you?"

"Leave off." Mama stooped over to smell a ragged rose growing in her "garden," the center of an oversized tractor tire. "Roland's a genius. That's what those school people said."

"Genius, my foot," Granny said as she was fixing to settled into her cracked vinyl chair out on the front porch under an awning. She stood there for a while until she could get her knees to bend and then sort of fell backwards into the packed foam recliner. A puff of air squeezed out between the punctures like exhaust from a car.

"You got a way about you, Roland," Mama turned to me. "I can see it in your eyes, a hunger. No, I always knew you were different." A red-winged blackbird in wild-growing shrubs caught Mama's eye. It scratched around in the dry summer leaves, setting up a commotion.

"You can say that again," Granny interjected.

Mama started up again. "Your mind is like a deep pond. Anything I or anyone else throws in doesn't even make a ripple. What you need is heavier things to be plunked in."

I knew what Mama meant. I was different. Different from Gary, my oldest brother living up in Vinton County with his wife and kids, or Larry, who, like Daddy, was always fiddling with motors. Thank God I had nothing in common with my sister Angie, who lived in town with her husband and worked at the Curl Up and Dye hair salon. Angie would just as soon slap you as to look at you. She was meaner than dirt, dirtier than a dog, and doggone difficult to boot.

"Now, Roland." Mama always started her sentences slowly. It embarrassed me when she did this because regular people—not family—would start to talk over her or finish her thought for her, sometimes saying for Mama what she didn't mean at all. "Make me proud, son. This is your chance. Do good and you'll go places."

For the longest time I hadn't noticed we were poor. We had everything we needed, it seemed. Wind blew at us, snow fell, rain tried to get in, but we were always safe. We'd gotten electricity, which was better than most of our neighbors. And, a couple of years ago the county had come out and strung up telephone wires, crisscrossing the hills like tic-tac-toe.

I'm not sure when, but eventually I became aware. We didn't live like most folk. Someday I was going to leave, escape the ridge our trailer straddled in the foothills of the Appalachians. When I grew up I was going to follow those looping telephone lines. To Cincinnati, Columbus, maybe Chicago.

Daddy pulled into the gravel square in the front yard in his truck. He'd been to the recycling center. My family took more stuff away from the dump than contributed to it. Most of his finds ended up strewn across our hillside after it was determined they were unfixable and truly junk. After getting himself a beer and settling into the couch he asked to see my new school books. I opened my book bag. Granny pretended to be asleep in her chair, but kept sneaking peeks with one eye open.

Larry whistled through his teeth. "Shiny, ain't they."

Daddy picked up an American history textbook and turned it over as if it was a revolver about to go off. "Seems heavy," he said.

He put down the book and with a solemn look on his creased and sun-browned face said, "Now Roland, don't go giving anybody any trouble at that new school or you'll hear it from me."

"Yes, sir," I answered him.

After dinner Daddy asked me to come help him water the crops. First we had to fill up trash barrels in the back of Daddy's truck from the garden hose. Before leaving we threw in several empty plastic milk jugs. We drove on out to the blacktop and picked up the main road going south. The hot day was melting into long shadows. I loved this time when finally there was relief from the heat. Orange tiger lilies growing wild in the ditches beside the road swayed in the evening breeze. It was as if the land were letting go, unclenching its fist.

Without meaning to, I sighed.

Daddy glanced at me from beneath his greasy cap. "What's the matter with you?"

"Nothing."

Talking to Daddy was like tuning in a radio station late at night—one minute it's coming in loud and clear and the next minute you've lost it and the room is filled with static.

He shook his head and returned his eyes to the road. "What a wonder you are, Roland," he said after a few minutes of silence.

A mile later he forked off the county highway and carefully picked his way along a deeply rutted road so as not to spill the bed-load of water. The track seemed to lead to nowhere, and ten minutes later we came to a dead end at the edge of a thick woods.

Now for the real work. As soon as we got out, a cool musky odor swamped us, an odd smell of old and fresh, things long dead and things brand new. We dipped and filled our milk jugs from the barrels and began the walk to the crop-patch.

In order for our family to get by, Daddy needed a get-rich-quick crop, and the only thing paying was marijuana. I knew it was wrong, and it didn't make it any righter that most of the county people were doing the same thing. But the fact that "everyone was doing it" made it not seem so bad. It was how we got money for the things we needed, like a new shower stall to replace the green, mildewed one.

When we entered the murky, overripe forest, I nearly lost my load when I tripped over a washed-out tree root.

"Careful, boy," Daddy barked at me.

"Sorry," I apologized, and kept on going.

When selecting where to plant, Daddy had to be careful, because the sheriff used a single-engine plane to fly over the hills searching for growers. If it looked like someone had obviously cleared a patch, then it would have been a tip off. So Daddy hid his patch deep beneath a canopy of trees.

Water swished out and splashed off the toe of my tennis shoe. Something shiny glinted. I stooped to pick it up.

"Whoa!" I called out to Daddy. "An arrowhead." I'd read about arrowheads in a book about Daniel Boone. "Indians used these to hunt buffalo, bear, wolves, and all the other long-gone game. This arrowhead might have been used by some young warrior to kill a panther."

"Ain't no panthers."

"Used to be," I said.

"Let me see that." Daddy took it from me and tried to examine it in the scant light. "Collectors pay top dollar for these. Anything relating to the Indian is worth money these days."

All of a sudden I felt a whoosh as if some ancient breath had breathed on me. The hair on the nape of my neck stood up. For a moment I pictured a red-skinned father and son standing where we were now, before the white man came, before the buffalo got killed off, before the big, old trees all got cut down. Goosebumps went up and down my arms. "They're here, now, with us," I incanted in a spooky voice.

Daddy stepped back, startled, but regained his senses. "Roland, I swear. What the hell are you talking about?"

"Ghosts."

Like opening a faucet, out of my mouth sloshed some lines from *Hiawatha*, a poem I'd learned at school:

> *By the shores of Gitche Gumee,*
> *By the shining Big-Sea-Water,*
> *Stood the wigwam of Nokomis*
> *Daughter of the Moon, Nokomis.*
> *Dark behind it rose the forest—*

"Stop!" Daddy shouted, grabbing my arm. "Stop it, I say. You—you—" He sputtered, his breath coming out in strangled chokes. His eyes moistened and he blinked rapidly to clear them.

"Daddy, are you okay?"

He handed me back the arrowhead and picked up his jugs. "Let 'em rest," he said, continuing down the dim trail.

Just as we were going over a rise Daddy gasped and snatched my bucket to the ground. "Get down," he whispered hoarsely.

We crouched low. Every last plant had been pulled up and trampled, crushed under foot. My heart beat so loud I wrapped my arms around my chest trying to muffle the sound.

Suddenly I was okay with our cracked and green shower stall, just as long as we could go home and not to jail. The sheriff or county agents must have come out and destroyed the crop.

"High-tail it," Daddy ordered in a low voice.

He and I slowly backed up and took off running. I glanced back once or twice to see if anyone was following us. By the time we reached the truck, Daddy was wheezing. I pounded him on the back as he bent over double fighting for air. After a couple of minutes he straightened up and wiped his mouth on the bottom of his yellowed white T-shirt.

"I'm sorry, Daddy— "I tried to say.

"Hush!" he wheezed, holding onto the door handle for support. "Get in the truck."

Back home, I sat on the porch in Granny's vinyl chair while Mama and Daddy scrunched up against one another on the couch watching TV inside. I squinted at my parents through the screen door. Blue smoke from Daddy's cigarette curled upward.

"Sorry about your crop," Mama whispered.

Daddy reached his scrawny arms around Mama, not quite all the way around since she was of good size, and gave her a hug. "S'kay, darlin'." Mama giggled, not loud enough to wake Granny.

In the side bedroom Granny snored loud enough to scare away the bats flitting around in the nighttime sky. Granny was a fitful sleeper, often calling out, leave off! or screaming for unseen hands to let go.

Far off down the road I heard a neighbor's dog howl. Its mournful cry made me lonelier than anything. Nearby, crickets chirped from between cracks in the cement. A sort of drowsy gloom crept over me.

Over the summer I'd read *Great Expectations*. Pip, the orphan boy, didn't fit into his family either. He was desperate to get away, leave his village and go off to London and live like a gentleman. I fingered the arrowhead in my pocket.

A dew-mist rose up from the ground. Like a lady's shawl, it settled upon the surrounding foot-hills and night-trees, shrouding the cars up on blocks, draping the junk in the yard and turning them into grey tombstones.

I pretended I was Pip in the graveyard wishing for a benefactor, someone to come save me. I needed to be rescued from my trailer trash life. I prayed aloud to a nameless prisoner: "Help me to get along better at school and make friends. Help Daddy to get work. And, sorry about the pot patch."

Freak Shows and
Ferris Wheels

Still at a distance, I could see the Ferris wheel towering above wilted stalks of corn. The wind carried the whirly-whizz and ching-ching and rat-a-tat-tat sounds of the carnival across the dusty fields. Larry had told me to come on out to the Athens Fall Festival and he'd get me on all the rides for free.

My heavy bike flew down the hills, loose gravel rattling inside its metal fenders. On the long uphill climb, my old ironclad slowed to a lumbering halt after only a minute. I got off and pushed it, salty sweat stinging my eyes. Shimmers of heat rose up from the baked asphalt like ghost angels.

The first thing I was going to do was slug back a Coke, then eat an elephant ear buried in powdered sugar.

Vroom! Out of nowhere a mini-bike gunned past me. Kyle Messerhoff with his big block head and green and white jersey laughed at me as he sped by.

"Jerk." I wiped my forehead with the sleeve of my T-shirt and got back on my bike.

If only I had a mini-bike. I'd asked Daddy for one last Christmas, but of course it was out of the question. Larry offered to build me one out of spare parts, but that, too, got nixed.

When I finally got to the county fairgrounds, I stashed my bike in some bushes and hit the midway on the look-out for Larry. Barkers called out to me to come play their games. *Knock 'em down, only a quarter, pick your prize!* I scanned the peg wall of ratty stuffed animals and sets of fuzzy "pair of dice" smooshed in next to a gigantic bear wearing a blue-checked bandana. Suddenly someone or something bopped me on top of the head from behind.

I turned to face Larry holding an inflatable hammer with a little jingle bell inside of it.

"Make you wet your pants, did I?" Larry laughed, sounding just like the balloon hammer when you squeezed it.

"No, Larry. You startled me, that's all."

Larry busted up again, fit to split his twig body in two. He was about six-foot-two and weighed maybe one hundred and thirty pounds. "Boy, you shoulda seen your face." He doubled over.

"Aren't you supposed to be working?"

"Yeah, but a man need a break ever' once in a while. C'mon, I'll show you around."

We skipped the long line out front of a huge circus tent and crawled under the heavy canvas. It took a minute for my eyes to adjust to the dimness and when they did I jumped backwards. In front of us was a man with a thousand tattoos swallowing a coat hanger.

Larry winked at me. "I'm always kidding him about his bad breath," he said. Larry gave the guy a jesting elbow in the ribs. The coat hanger swallower gagged, exhaling the hanger.

Larry introduced me. "This is my kid brother Roland, the one I told you about.

"The smart one?" the man asked, wiping rusty saliva from his lips with the back of his hand. He extended his hand toward me. "Larry's always bragging on how smart you are."

I didn't want to shake, but he grabbed my hand anyway.

A second later Larry was pulling me toward the

other end of the tent. "I want you to see somethin'. It's a miracle, it is." Larry threw back a sheet covering a large cage.

I peered inside. "What is it, Larry?"

From behind a curtain, a man announced with increasing excitement the biggest, the weirdest, "the never-before seen and never will again—"

A white-feathered form scratched around in the dirty straw. Where the bird's head should have been was a crusted-over stump. There were no eyes, no beak, and no wobbly red thing under its chin. Heck, there was no chin, just neck and body.

"The one, the only, ladies and gentlemen—" A burst of applause exploded.

"Holy cow," was all I could say.

"No," Larry said, sounding disappointed that I still didn't get it. "It's a headless chicken."

The bird lifted up on its taloned-toes and mutely rustled its wings.

"Some lady out Jackson way brought it in. Said she'd chopped its head off and it run around the barnyard. Tweren't nothing unusual about that except it didn't lay down and die. It just kept on running. She caught it when it got snagged in some bushes and put it in a sack. When the next morning it was still alive she carried it over here. The man in charge of the show paid her twenty dollars for her chicken."

"How's it eat?" The thing settled back onto the straw.

"Dunno. But so far it's lived a week. Cool, ain't it?"

I was grossed out, while at the same time I couldn't turn away. Larry dragged me out into the bright sunlight and rainbow-colors of the midway. "Now I gotta go," he said, digging into his jeans pocket. "Here's five dollars. Go buy yourself whatever you want. And let me know if you need anything, okay?"

"Wow! Thanks Larry."

I followed the smell of hot fry-oil to the elephant ear vendor. Along the way I bought the biggest Coke I could find. When I found the elephant ear truck I told the guy behind the window I was Larry Tanner's brother. He shook powdered sugar over my order until it looked like a cow pie in a snow drift.

I took the paper plate limp with grease. "Man, oh, man." I started walking and eating in an elephant ear ecstasy, not paying much attention until—SMACK— right into a green and white wall. The plate flipped and dumped powdered sugar all down the front of Kyle.

"What the—hey!" He shook his shirt and sugar wafted up like a smoke fire. Kyle had maybe thirty pounds on me. He raised his hands as if to choke me or rattle me by the neck.

I didn't want to stand around to see what he might do. I dove into the dense crowd, weaving in between mamas with strollers and around packs of giggling girls and guys slamming down mallets and boinging bells. I raced past the merry-go-round where the calliope belted out a syncopated version of "Little Brown Jug" and past the Himalaya where the riders screamed when the contraption shifted into reverse and plunged backwards and upside down for thirty seconds. I spied what looked like a lopsided double-wide and quickly ducked into the Hall of Mirrors.

Inside I was thrust into a maze of Rolands all wondering where to go next. I'd accidentally entered through the exit so I had to push upstream against a throng of people coming from the opposite direction. "Watch out, stupid kid!"

I looked back to see if Kyle was following me and stared into the face of a midget. I opened my mouth to scream, until I realized it was me. Next I felt my way around a dark corner. How did I know some lady was standing there? I might've given her a little feel because all of a sudden her handbag came down hard on my head. The Hall of Mirrors was turning into a House of Horrors. I had to get out of there!

A few more bumps and twists and I escaped out the entrance into the blinding sunlight.

Squinting, I caught a glimpse of Larry and the Tilt-a-Whirl and sprinted to the front of the line. "Can I go next?" I blurted.

The ride had just ended and Larry was fixing to release a new set of customers.

"Okay, little buddy, but you got to double up. This line ain't getting any shorter. Any of you solo?" he bellowed loud enough for the last person in line to hear.

"Me!" cried a squeaky voice.

Oh, no. Hassan.

"Whatever, get in." Larry waved us both into the corral.

I jumped in into an open car and Hassan pulled the safety bar into place. The carriage lurched as the ride started up.

"I don't like this." Hassan's eyes were as big as blackberries. "Is it safe?"

"I guess." I'd never thought about it. There was a pretty wide gap that puny guys like us could slip through and hurtle to our death.

We started out slow going around and around. I spotted Kyle down below. He had a big grease spot on his shirt like a bull's eye. Powdered sugar frosted his square head. He shook his fist at us as we flew by.

"What's going on?" asked Hassan.

I shrugged as if it was a complete mystery.

The velocity increased and I could feel my cheeks shake. We were going faster, so fast the car tilted as it whirled around. At one point we were totally perpendicular to the ground.

My intestines twisted. It felt like I'd swallowed a coat hanger. Something caught in my gullet. I burped and it tasted like sugary grease.

We boomeranged along rising and falling as the knot in my stomach tightened, squeezing whatever was inside of me up the chimney of my windpipe. I was about to say Whoa! when a slew of carnival food erupted.

Chunks of regurgitated elephant ear mixed in with some mysterious pink fluid hung in the air as if weightless, like a scarf waving in the wind. Then gravity kicked in and the mess rained down on the upturned face of Kyle.

Hassan scooted to the farthest edge of the swinging seat, his blackberry eyes about to burst.

The last I saw of Kyle was the back of his Bobcat jersey as he ran off, the crowds gladly parting.

"Sorry," I managed to say, wiping my mouth on the hem of my T-shirt.

Hassan blinked back a wordless reply. I think we were both a bit stunned.

On the next swing through I gave Larry a thumbs-up to let him know I was going to be okay. I guess he was right—it should be called the Tilt-a-Hurl.

The ride slowed until it crept along. I pushed against the bar. For being all worried about safety, the latch was sticky. Hassan reached over and with a flick of his finger released it.

A rush of little kids, Larry's next victims, streamed inside the enclosure, running around looking for empty cars.

I hopped down. There was no sign of Kyle. Maybe he was plotting something even grosser to get back at me.

Larry came up and slapped me on the back. "What's up, Chuck!"

Before disappearing, I scuffed the ground, keeping my eyes focused on my holy sneakers. "See you at school on Monday," I told Hassan.

He nodded without smiling. I guess we were both a bit like freak show headless chickens, just trying to survive.

5

Anne Frank Teaches
Us a Lesson

In English we were starting to read *The Diary of Anne Frank*, actually a play adapted from the diary. Ms. Knudsen asked that we each write a one-page essay of what struck us personally from our reading. The class moaned, all except Patty, who raised her hand to ask if it needed to be typed, and a kid named Riley McGuire, who asked about word count.

Anne seemed like a silly girl, I mean, come on—*Dear Kitty!*—writing about film stars and boyfriends. But I doubted I could write that in my report.

Ms. Knudsen decided to have us work in pairs in order to "bounce" ideas off one another. I silently prayed I'd get assigned to Patty, but no such luck. She put Hassan and me together.

We went to the school library where we sat at a corner table for a long time without talking. Finally Hassan spoke up.

"I'm not sure I get it. This seems like a girl thing."

I couldn't believe he said that. It was exactly what I'd been thinking.

"Anne reminds me of my sisters," he went on. "They are constantly talking about movie stars. All over the walls of their bedroom are posters of Shaun Cassidy and Donny Osmond. Who is Donny Osmond?"

"He sings on a variety show my Mom and Grandma watch on TV. He's crap," I said.

Hassan shook his head. "Girls like such frivolous things. They act like they know it all and then complain that you never help. One minute giggling over a phone call and the next unhappy about—" For a second he seemed lost and then shrugged. "—about what, I don't know."

I knew exactly what he was talking about. Though not a giggler, my sister Angie was either ignoring me or wanting to beat me up. She didn't take nothing off no one.

"Why can't we do a book report on *Jaws*?" Hassan mused aloud.

"Right! Now you're talking. I read that book this past summer and, afterwards, I didn't shower for a week." I'd never really had a conversation with someone my own age about books. Teachers and librarians didn't count.

I remember when I first learned to read. We used to live in a two-room shack down by the railroad tracks. I liked to wake up with the birds when the morning sky was the color of dirty bathwater with little slivers of soap clouds floating in it. I had to be real quiet because Daddy was sleeping after working a graveyard shift, which I reckoned at the time meant he worked in a cemetery.

Since I was the only one awake, I had to amuse myself. So I would look at newspaper pasted to the bare pine boards in the corner of the bedroom I shared with Angie, Gary and Larry. A summer storm had torn off the tar paper on the outside of the house and Daddy had tried to repair it by nailing up flattened tin and stuffing the cracks with newspaper. After a season the paper had yellowed and was brittle around the edges. One morning I got up and was studying a news picture of a car with its front end bashed in and a woman lying off to the side.

There were marks under the picture. I traced them with my finger until I finally deciphered what they meant.

"Logan woman car crash."

"*What?*" Angie flung the covers off her face. With her hair every which way she reminded me of a scarecrow.

"Logan woman," I said again, pointing to the black and yellow picture on the wall.

Angie sat up. Her eyes narrowed to a slit. "Who been teaching you to read?"

"Nobody," I said. I was afraid she might smack me upside the head. "I just figured it out on my own. See, this here is Logan, that's where Daddy works. And this word is car and this other'n is cr—ash. Crash!"

"You're just making this up." She said it like she was mad. "What about this word?" She tested me by having me read from other parts of the wall. Some words I got right, some she had to help me with, but most of them I sounded out on my own.

Eventually Angie slid back down under the sheets. "If'n you know what's good for you, you'll stop reading because once you get old like me it'll hurt your brain."

But I didn't stop. I kept going, racing down the shelves of the school library, eventually working my way alphabetically through the Ds. So far.

"Where do we start?" Hassan ripped a clean sheet of lined paper out of his spiral notebook.

I had no idea.

"It's hard to believe they hid for so long. How many months were they hiding?" Hassan asked.

"Two and a half years," I answered. "I've often wondered why people didn't rise up against Hitler earlier? Like couldn't they have just voted him out?"

"It's not always easy to get rid of a bad leader. My uncle under the Shah—"

"The Shah?"

"He was the monarch of Iran. My uncle—"

"Was?" I was confused.

"Yes, he was—how do you say—he left."

"Dethroned?" I guessed.

"He was a bad man. Some of my parents' friends were arrested for criticizing the Shah. The prisons were full. Iran is not like America where you can say almost anything and not get into trouble. In Iran it is illegal to disagree. My uncle is a professor of political science and he explained to me. The Shah's secret police had eyes and ears everywhere. We were—" Hassan's eyes darted around the library then leaned in toward me. "Always wondering who is a friend, who is the enemy."

The librarian at her desk gave us a cold stare. I was hoping she wouldn't come over to shush us. She was nice, but had dog breath, and, because she talked in a low voice, she always got up close.

"Anyway," Hassan went on, "my uncle was arrested."

I thought I was the only kid at Athens Middle School whose relatives had been in jail.

"My parents do not speak of it."

I knew what he meant. We weren't too proud either.

"He was tortured, but at least he is alive. Last summer was the worst. Every day there were protests in the streets. Many of the cinemas closed."

"That's bad." I said.

"Lots of people were killed. It got to the point my parents decided to apply to leave, so that my father may further his studies."

"What about your uncle?" I asked. Over Hassan's shoulder I glimpsed Patty and Kyle working together.

"He has stayed to help with the new government since the Shah was driven out, forced to leave the country."

"So," I began, "where is this, the Shah, now?"

"Here! In America!" Hassan said, his voice rising.

The school librarian walked past our table and held her finger up to her lips. "Boys," she whispered sternly.

Hassan lowered his voice. "My father says this will not turn out well."

I watched as Patty and Kyle gathered up their

notebooks. I really liked Patty's teeth. When she smiled I felt a rush, like a fast car—different, though, than Larry at the wheel. More like speeding with the windows rolled down. Kyle must have noticed me staring. He glared at me.

It had been hard to walk back from that scene where I'd thrown up on him at the fair. There was no chance he was ever going to forget or forgive me. And, there was no chance I could ever defend myself by saying nature was just taking its course. I couldn't have planned revenge any better than nailing him that afternoon. Still, I was always careful around him. I definitely steered clear of him at lunch. Though I couldn't do anything about gym class where he gunned for me at dodgeball. I got hit in the head with the ball so many times by Kyle I felt like I was one giant target.

Glancing down at the blank sheet of paper in front of us, I asked Hassan, "Will you go back?"

"Of course, it is our country. Now Iran is a democracy, just like the U.S. And soon we will hold elections."

Patty stopped by our table and smiled. "Hey guys! How's it going?"

"Not the greatest," I responded, hoping she might sit down, help us crack this Anne Frank thing wide open.

"What were you laughing about?" she asked.

Hmmm. I think it was how ridiculous girls are. "Uh, nothing."

Patty wiggled her fingers in goodbye to us. In her wake was a scent: clean, like fresh-cut grass or celery. As she disappeared around a corner I wished . . . I wished for so much. I couldn't even describe what it was.

"It would be hard for me," I began, shifting the conversation back to Anne Frank, "to stay cooped up for so long. I'd have to bust out."

I imagined Anne Frank secretly writing in a narrow, shared space, much like a crowded, cluttered trailer, having no real place of her own.

"Anne Frank was so naive and optimistic." Hassan shook his head. "How could she possibly dream of a better world?"

Anne Frank reminded me of Mama and her tractor-tire garden.

"Maybe," I started up, not sure where I was going with my next thought. "Hope isn't such a bad thing. It can keep a person going, make life, even a crazy, mixed-up life, a little more bearable."

Hassan picked up his pencil. "That's good. Let's start there."

Of Ghosts and Next-of-Kin

It was time for Larry to go work the carnival circuit. He loaded the rusted-out Impala with an ice chest full of beer and threw a garbage bag of clothes into the backseat.

"Take care of yourself, Roland," he said. "Don't do anything I wouldn't do." He winked and messed up my hair.

No problem there, Larry, I might have said, but instead waved goodbye as he pulled out in a plume of dust.

For all his wild and unpredictable ways, Larry was fun to have around. The place seemed quieter, emptier without him.

It was October and the hills were a patchwork of green and gold, red and orange. At night the cold made the trailer pop when the aluminum walls that had heated up during the day contracted. Mornings were crisp and fresh like biting into a just-picked apple. Now that the weather was getting cooler, I pulled Granny's old vinyl rocker in off the front porch.

At school everyone was getting ready for Halloween. Dancing skeletons and toothy pumpkins made out of colored paper decorated the walls of the classrooms. Patty headed up a decorating committee for a costume party to be held in the gymnasium.

The concept of dressing up for Halloween was new to me. Out in the boondocks kids didn't trick or treat. I tried to imagine some innocent kid dressed up like a lamb or an angel going door-to-door, or rather trailer-to-trailer, and Granny scaring the living daylights out of him, cussing up a storm and driving that boy or girl off the ridge. No, it would never have worked. Real life was scarier than the playful ghosts and smiling goblins strung up in the classrooms.

On the other hand, the chance to dress up like someone other than who I was appealed to me. I wondered what it would be like to put on a pair of shoulder pads and a football jersey and be Kyle Messerhoff.

On Halloween Eve the sun sank quickly behind the frosted hills which reminded me of white-sheeted ghosts. Feeling restless, I got up to close the off-kilter screen door.

"What's the matter with you?" Granny woke up. "Sit down. You're making me nervous."

"Thought I heard something, that's all." Maybe it was Daddy getting back from running some metal he'd "found" to a scrapper. Daddy liked to explore old abandoned buildings and pull out pipes, boilers, and such to redeem for cash.

"Nothin' but the neighbor's dog. If it were me I'd shoot that mutt, always disturbing the peace."

"Now, Granny." I tried to shush her before she got herself riled up.

"Don't 'now Granny' me, buster. It's this weather that's got me rattled. One day hotter than blazes and the next colder than hell." She stopped a minute to consider what she'd said. She went on, "Anyway sort of spooks a person, you know, all this Halloween business. When I was a kid we didn't need no Halloween, the hills were haunted enough. Growing up in West Virginia, you couldn't throw a rock without hitting the ghost of some dead Civil War veteran or the bloody specter of a woman murdered by her husband."

I shivered. "Quit, Granny."

"Listen to what I say," she said in an eerie voice. "There are saints and angels and spirits all around us, ever'where we go. You can't get away from them. They're always there, like air and clouds, mist and fog."

I felt one of Granny's tales coming on—one part ghost story, one part mountain myth, and a whole lot of nonsense in between.

"Back in West Virginia my cousin Junior worked the mines over Piedmont way on the Ohio side of the river. He'd work all week long, but come Sunday he would hike on over to my Ma and Pa's house not too far away. I reckon I was about fourteen or fifteen years old at the time. He had to cross the Ohio River at a particular bridge. I've forgotten the name of that bridge."

"Martin's Ferry, Granny." I had only heard this story about nine hundred times.

"Well if you knew it, why'd you ask me?" Her voice was keen, but her eyes were blurred over. She was somewhere else.

"One day he asked a fella he worked with, another coal miner, if he wanted to come with for a good home-cooked meal. He came for dinner that week and the week after that and then the week after that. Every Sunday he showed up and ate up all the ham and apple pie. T'weren't one thing left after Jedidiah Hodges was done eating. My ma liked that.

"I didn't, though. I thought he was a brazen man to come onto our part of the mountain. We were thirteen children on the place and all of us had to fight for a scrap at the dinner table. Maybe Ma and Pa had so many youngins because they were trying to even out the girls with the boys. I don't know, but their first six were girls. I was the oldest so I had to watch all the youngins and also be my father's son. I knew right well enough how hard food was to come by, but my Ma would've just as soon as stabbed me with a fork if I reached for the last piece of cornbread before offering it to a guest. 'Company gets firsts and lasts,' she'd always say and turn on me the evil eye."

I knew that look. I'd seen Granny cast it my way plenty of times.

"Well, I'd already done thought things out. If this kept up I'd starve to death. So I told Mama not to worry, that I was going to fix the meal the next time Jedidiah came. Mama musta thought I was sweet on him as I scurried around collecting apples, cracking walnuts, and rooting up potatoes and turnips.

"Sweet on him, nothin'." Granny made a harrumphing noise. "I was no sweeter on him than I was the man in the moon. There was one boy down in the valley that I had a hankerin' for, Gertie Haywood, the preacher's son, but he up and ran off with Wanda Puck from Silver Creek.

"No, I had another thing in mind for Jedidiah Hodges. There weren't no ham meat left in the smoke house, but the day before, I'd accidentally caught a 'possum in my trap. I skinned it and gutted it and boiled it up in a pot and served it to the stranger. Jedidiah ate it up, so as not to insult me. In fact, he complimented me on how good everything tasted. Maybe he'd caught on to the fact that I'd slipped him some peculiar meat because of the way I looked across the table and giggled at him. He was so nice. I sort of began to feel sorry for him. But not sorry enough not to wish he'd never come back."

I gazed into Granny's face, withered like a walnut hull. She wasn't as old as some grandmothers, but after her stomach operation and the hysterectomy, where they took out her womanly organs, she grew canyons, deep, across her cheeks and neck. Her wiry salt-and-pepper hair rarely got combed all the way through. To make it less flyaway she plastered it with hair oil that had the consistency of Crisco. Her eyes were dark and fierce, revealing a smidgen of that Cherokee Indian blood in her.

"From that day on he began to court me. He'd come over the river every Sunday to visit. We'd take a walk way back into the woods, maybe pick a passel of greens for supper or dig some wild ginseng, which—"

Here Granny straightened her shoulders. "Which beats scrappin' metal."

I paid her no mind.

"One time we discovered a cave. It smelled old and damp like something dead had crawled up inside of it. We made us a torch and crouched low so as not to knock our heads. He cast the light on the ceiling and it appeared to be moving. Upon closer inspection it was spiders, thousands of them, little white ones with no eyes, scurrying about like foam on a current."

I shuddered and brushed my hand over the back of my neck as if I were knocking off a dozen right then and there.

"To tell the truth, Jedidiah wasn't that handsome, but I pretended to like him. You see, I had plans. I wanted to get off that mountain—there was way too much work for one girl. Here was a man who had the means to get me away."

I understood Granny well enough on this account.

"Then something happened that told me I had better love him in earnest or forever be doomed.

"It was getting close to the weekend and I was expecting Jedidiah. It had been raining all that week, every day, and the creek that ran down front of the cabin was way up. Instead of a lazy whisper, it roared. I could hear it in my sleep as I waited for him."

"What happened to Jedidiah?" I asked, but I already knew the end of the story.

"Jedidiah was hell-bent to get across the river that night. Junior and the other men warned him that the river was high, too dangerous. But he was a fool for me." Granny pursed her lips, trying to hide a girlish smile.

"Anyway, he got to the bridge only to find a torrent. Water swirled around the cement posts that held it up. He got about halfway out when there was a loud crash and he felt the planks buckle beneath his feet, twist like they was dancing, turn, turn, turn. He clung to the metal railing as one by one the boards got ripped away by the rushing black water. Finally the railing was jerked out of his hands, and in he went.

"The cold, cold water stung him like needles and bruised him as he bobbed along before being sucked down. He fought the pull as best he could, but it was way too strong. The only thing he had to hold onto was the memory of me and my face.

"Out of nowhere he felt hands, wispy like tissue paper, but at the same time full of superhuman strength, grab him under his arms and tow him to the other side. He hauled himself up on the muddy bank and lay there panting for breath. After he'd hacked and spit to clear his lungs of river water and wiped his eyes, there stood before him a woman with long, long hair, naked as a jaybird with white, see-through skin. He recognized straight off that she t'weren't real but a ghost.

"'What do you want with me, lady?' he asked, thinking he'd survived drowning only to be murdered by a haunt.

"She told him of how she had lost her one true love, drowned in the Ohio River on a night such as this. She'd jumped in to save him, but was too late. They'd both gone under, never to surface again—until now. This was her last chance to redeem herself and save her soul from eternal wandering. She then disappeared, back into the night and drenching rain.

"He knew that his life had been spared for a purpose. He struggled up the long hill leading from the banks of the river and found the path up to our cabin. He burst through the door soaked to the bone, his teeth chattering to wake the dead. I flew outta bed and quick wrapped my quilt around him. I set him by the fire and began to boil water for coffee. It took a while, but once he'd warmed up and dried out a bit he told me the story. I didn't know whether to believe him or not, but what could I do? I couldn't right well defy destiny—I married him."

Once again the neighbor's dog started barking. I jumped up to see what the commotion was all about.

"Probably a coon or something," I said out loud if only to quiet my own nerves.

The moon loomed over the treetops big and full, casting long-fingered shadows.

Granny sniffed. "Ain't no coon. It's *her* come back again to punish me for leaving the mountain after Grandpa died," she whispered as her voice trailed off.

Headlights topped a hill before disappearing into a dip. Someone was coming down the road. I waited to see if they would pass by our place, but the car turned in, ghosted in a cloud of dust.

"Who's it, boy?" Mama called out from her room; she didn't like hearing Granny's stories.

A racket worse than dogs commenced from inside the automobile. "Not sure." It seemed as if the car was going to explode until the doors popped open and children swarmed out. A woman emerged from the passenger side with a baby slung over her shoulder.

I let out a moan and pressed my forehead against the screen. This was worse than courting ghosts or rag-a-muffin trick-or-treaters. My brother Gary and his family were a nightmare.

Crossing Fence Lines

They stayed. Or took over was more like it. The trailer wasn't really meant to sleep that many people. We had bodies everywhere, camped out on the floor, on the pull-out couch, and little ones side-by-side in Larry's top bunk since he was on the road.

There was Gary and his wife Jean whose bleached blonde hair turned orange in the bright sunlight. Then there were the girls, Jean's by a previous marriage: Brandy and Mandy, who hogged the bathroom and left big clumps of hair in the sink. The twins were Andy and Randy, tow-headed and lardy with mouths continually ringed with dirt or cookie or both. Within hours of arriving they'd managed to pull all the knobs off the television and smear the screen with their sticky hands. I hid my prize arrowhead between pages of my favorite paperback kept on a shelf by my bunk.

Worst of all was the baby, Gary Junior, who was a non-stop poop machine. Actually he ran from both ends—there was a double-barrel stream of green coming from his nose. Instead of crawling on all fours, the baby liked to scoot across the shag-carpet with one leg tucked up underneath him. He had rug burns on his bottom, where the meaty part of him hung out of his diaper.

I couldn't wait to escape the house the next morning.

At school the kids were all comparing their Halloween hauls and at lunch they bartered back and forth like it was a farm auction. Two Mars bars for a Baby Ruth. Zagnuts and Marathon bars were junk bonds. Hassan brought Reese's Cups and became the most popular kid in the cafeteria. He placed one beside my lunch tray, the kind with compartments for the main entrée and all the sides. There was even a circle impression for a cup where I wedged my milk carton.

"What's that for?" I asked, eyeing the Reese's in its orange and brown wrapper. "I don't have nothing to trade for it," I went on.

"It is freely given. No need to give me anything in return," Hassan answered.

His generosity, instead of making me happy, made me feel worse than ever.

"Thanks," I said, moving the Reese's to one of my empty compartments. "Reese's are my favorite candy bar."

Patty perched down beside us at the lunch table. "Hey you guys did a great job with your Anne Frank presentation."

"We got an A," bragged Hassan.

"Listen, I was wondering if you were interested in helping out with Thanksgiving decorations. I'm organizing a group that will meet after school next week in the art room."

"Sure," we both said.

After she walked away Hassan commented. "Patty is very nice."

I watched as she moved through the cafeteria, her blonde hair swaying. I couldn't agree with him more.

Walking into the trailer after school, I found the twins jumping on the couch and piling all the cushions onto the floor. A slab of sunlight dazzled with dust while cushion fluff floated down. I retreated to my bunk only to find the cover of my copy of *Great Expectations* ripped off, lying decapitated amongst my blankets. The arrowhead was missing.

"What the heck!" I stormed into the kitchen where the girls were making fudge. Several scorched pots occupied the stovetop while the sink overflowed with dirty dishes. They paid me no nevermind. "Which one of y'all stole my arrowhead?"

Brandy, the oldest and sassiest, stopped in the middle of licking a sludge-coated wooden spoon. "What arrowhead?"

Mandy, her mouth gooed with chocolate, pulled her head guiltily into her shoulders like a turtle.

I snatched the spoon out of Brandy's hand and threatened Mandy. "Where'd cha put it?"

"Mama!" the girls screamed and started making a dash for the trailer door just as Daddy and Gary tramped in from hunting wearing mud-sucker boots.

Daddy took one look at me wielding the spoon and the girls carrying on and said, "Boy, what's going on here?"

"These kids are driving me crazy getting into my stuff and wrecking everything," I railed.

Daddy sat down heavily on the naked couch. "We got us a buck!" Gary exclaimed.

Exhaustion ringed Daddy's eyes, making the saggy

pouches underneath look like crescent bruises. "Pull these boots off will ya, Roland."

I put the spoon down and immediately Brandy picked it up and continued cleaning it with her tongue.

"My arrowhead's gone," I said, yanking at the muddy boot. I could tell they'd been down in the ravine. "Make them give it back."

Instead of standing up for me, he wheezed, "Give me a minute, damn it, Roland." He leaned back into the cushion-less couch and closed his eyes. His nostrils flared and narrowed with each breath he drew. Just watching him made my own chest hurt.

I headed out of the trailer and down the ravine, across the creek, hopping over mossy stones spaced about a foot apart, following a faint deer path criss-crossed with downed trees. I bushwhacked through thick underbrush of buckthorn, jack oak brush, and purple vines that smacked me in the back as I pushed through. Nail-like prickers and spiked burrs snagged the nylon of my windbreaker.

Out of breath and bleeding from where the wild grape vines had scratched me, I paused by a random boulder, glistening with flecks of quartz. Dragged there, I reckoned, by the ebb and flow of glaciers eons ago. I passed a lone tree stripped of its leaves and bark with its pale belly exposed. On the trunk were strange marks, hieroglyphics engraved by bore-beetles.

In the middle of a stand of fir trees was a small clearing. Here was quiet. I dropped down upon a bed of soft pine needles and stared up through the boughs at patchy blue sky.

My daddy was a lot like crossing fence lines. He always told me to be careful when out walking. *Don't cross fence lines*, he'd warn. You might not ever find your way back. There's no telling where you might end up. That's how it was with Daddy. I had no idea of where I stood with him, no point of reference.

Gary and Daddy got along great, sipping beers together in the front seat of the pickup or sitting in the woods with their shotguns waiting for a deer or some unsuspecting animal to step into their view. Daddy never seemed happier than when he and Larry had their heads stuck up inside the hood of a car. Me—I was miserable at mechanics. Worse than any multiple-choice test was Daddy asking me to hand him a tool. I'd invariably hand him the wrong kind. *No, boy, not the Philips, the flat head one.* Daddy would shake his head as if I'd handed him a snake instead of a screwdriver.

We were like oil and water. No matter how much I tried to mix in, be like the others, I sunk to the bottom. At school I was just as much a foreigner as Hassan, while at home I was an alien.

I must've drifted off laying on the soft ground because I woke up clammy and cold, in gray twilight. I managed to make my way out of the clearing and across the creek with the help of cloudless moonlight. Walking back up from the ravine, I prayed the bathroom would be free and I could warm up in a hot shower. Still outside the door I heard the voices of six or seven different conversations rising and falling on the wind. The TV blared and the baby Gary Junior screamed as if his legs were being sawn off. I pried open the screen door hanging by its one hinge.

Mama, Daddy, and Gary sat on the couch watching TV, which wasn't unusual except it was tuned to the news. "What's going on?" I asked.

"It's a special report. There's been some sort of attack," Daddy said.

I sat down on the floor in front of Mama's legs, still wearing my coat. My hand squished something sticky matted onto the carpet.

"What?" I asked, smelling my hand. "Where?"

Gary shook his head. "Iran, they say, but I've never heard of it."

A chilled apprehension came over me. "It's in the Middle East." Fuzzy images flitted across the screen.

The news flashed a picture of an old man with a funny-shaped black hat. He had long gray whiskers and what Granny would call the evil eye. A mob of angry dark-haired boys hardly older than Hassan had taken over the U. S. Embassy in Tehran. Walter Cronkite the newscaster described the protesters as students.

Why would students want to take over an embassy? And why were they burning an American flag?

The bathroom door opened and Brandy and Mandy came out with their heads wrapped in towels. I was certain the shower drain was clogged and all the hot water was gone.

Captured embassy workers were paraded before the camera while the crowd held up signs. DOWN WITH INFIDELS, DOWN WITH AMERICA. Black shrouded women let loose with a weird noise that sounded like a turkey gobble.

Jean deposited Gary Junior on Gary's lap. The baby smelled like it had messed its pants.

"Why's they called gorillas?" Mama said, taking the baby.

"It's not what you're thinking Mama. A guerilla is like a rebel." But what did I know. It was all so confusing.

Mama let the baby slide off her lap to crawl around on the floor.

Granny startled herself out of a catnap. "Look who's back," she said, grimacing at me.

I expected the girls to surround me with their beehive-towel hairdos and bust out in the gobble-gobble noise. The baby scooted next to me and began to suck the jelly off the carpet.

"You should have been with us today," Daddy started up. "We got us a big buck. What do you reckon Gary, about two-eighty?" Daddy said, referring to the weight.

"Bigger'n that, I 'spect." Gary sat tugging at his little chin beard.

We don't even speak the same language, I thought. I got up to grab clean clothes from the footlocker under my bed. In the spare light from the TV I spied something on my pillow. The arrowhead.

An Eighth-Grade Infidel

Early the next morning Gary and Jean and their brood of children loaded up and left. I moved a pile of damp towels off my school books and waited out front for the school bus.

Once at school, I went to the library to see if there was a newspaper where I could read for myself what was going on. Bold headlines proclaimed: **U.S. Embassy Taken, Americans Held Hostage**. In the article the words students, militants, and terrorists were all used interchangeably. Pictures showed the hostages blindfolded with their hands bound at the wrists.

Hassan quietly took a seat at the table where I was sitting.

"Oh, hey," I said, trying to refold the newspaper, only managing to crumple it. I gave up and attempted a lame pun. "I don't see what this embassy thing has to do with us. I mean the Middle East ain't middle school."

Hassan reacted in a heartbeat. "It has everything to do with us. Nothing happens in the world that doesn't in some way affect others."

"Sorry, I just meant—." My voice trailed off.

Kids filed past us on their way to lockers and homeroom.

"This place—Tehran—are you from there?" I asked.

Hassan answered, this time taking a second. "Yeah, but it wasn't quite like this—at least not that I was aware of. My family—we aren't radicals. We had parties, big feasts where we all got together. I went to school, played football, what you call soccer. We even went out for fast food. You know, Kentucky Fried Chicken."

It all sounded normal to me.

"The Ayatollah—"

"The guy with dark caterpillar eyebrows?" I'd seen pictures of him on TV. He claimed the United States was the Great Satan.

"The Ayatollah Khomeini," Hassan continued, "is a very important religious leader."

"Like Billy Graham?"

Hassan went on. "For many years he lived in exile because he spoke out against the Shah. Only recently he has returned."

I glanced around to see if anyone was listening.

"For years the Shah and his family grew rich from the oil fields. The Queen was constantly redecorating the royal palace. I know from my uncle that the Shah had abolished political parties. His security chiefs made sure that no one opposed him. He jailed and killed many of his top political rivals. Don't get me wrong, Roland. I'm very sorry about the embassy workers. I don't agree with what the students are doing or what the Ayatollah is saying. But don't you see—we needed a revolution."

I wished he'd keep his voice down.

"According to my uncle, many people are distrustful of the United States because they have pledged support for the Shah. He's here in the States right now for medical treatment, but many believe it is a lie. That he is not sick at all. They think the U.S. is plotting to overthrow Iran."

I suddenly realized how this situation must look. Here I was sitting at the same table with an Iranian, the very people chanting "Death to America." I didn't want the other kids to think I was somehow guilty by association. So far I'd been able to keep my head down and not attract much attention. That's how I wanted it.

I coughed. "Hey, this is interesting, but I've got to go."

"Where?"

"Homeroom."

Hassan checked his wristwatch. "I'll go with you." Hassan was like a sticky booger. I just couldn't shake him.

"But first I have to go to the bathroom," I lied, not wanting to be seen with him. "You know, an emergency."

He continued looking up at me, his brow washboarded with lines of confusion.

"Meet you there," I said, hurrying to get away.

In homeroom after roll call the squirrel-faced teacher took a minute to discuss current events with the class. "I guess you've all heard what's going on?"

Kyle spoke without raising his hand. "I think America ought to go over there and whip Khomeini's ass." The class all started talking at once.

The teacher tried to quiet the classroom. "Now Kyle, let's not use inciteful language."

Kyle beamed. He must have thought she meant *insightful*.

"I think Americans should be careful not to blame all Iranians for what a few have done," Patty said.

Kyle faked a loud yawn.

I glanced at Hassan. His big eyes seemed bigger

than ever this morning, flecked with fear. He cast them down as if preoccupied by the books on his desk.

After homeroom, while heading out the door, Patty asked if she could walk with me to our next class.

"Uh, yeah." I was surprised it was a question.

"I'm glad you and Hassan are friends," she confided in me.

I noticed a few stray strands of hair clinging to her maxi-gloss lips. I was tempted to reach up and tuck the hair behind her ear.

She continued. "I think he needs us—"

Kyle strolled up behind Patty and thumped her on the shoulder. "Are we still meeting after school to work on those Thanksgiving decorations?"

She turned to me. "You're helping, too, right?"

Get together, with Patty?

Kids streamed around us as if we were a logjam in the middle of a creek. Behind her, Kyle sneered at me, curling his lip, showing his front teeth, oversized just like the rest of him. I hesitated, and then slowly answered, "Sure."

Twice a week we had shop class where we learned to measure and re-measure and put pencil marks on two by fours indicating where the shop teacher should make his cuts. We weren't allowed to run the saws.

The woodshop instructor was also the school football coach, and he taught the class the same way he gave orders on the football field.

"Tanner, Roland. Clean up that sawdust. NOW. You there with the baggy drawers, wipe that smirk off your face before I knock it off."

Mr. Koslowski acted tough, like he was on top of all his players. In truth he was blind to half of what went on in his class. For example, instead of making paperweights that looked like bobcats, the Athens Middle School mascot, Kyle and the rest of the football team were actually manufacturing wooden handguns for rubber band wars. Each guy customized his gun for a comfortable finger fit and notched it to hold a thick rubber band.

"What is this supposed to be, Messerhoff?" Mr. Koslowski demanded.

"It's a bobcat, sir." Kyle stood as if at attention and answered military-style.

Mr. K turned the gun over in his hand, examining it. "It looks like a gun to me," he said. He had the look of a man that could easily change his mind.

"You see, sir, it's a bobcat gun *to be used as* a paperweight."

He gave Kyle an approving nod. "Good job, son. Keep up the good work."

Hassan and I looked up from our side of the worktable where we were filing our paperweights into weird wooden blobs.

"You, Hassan," Mr. Koslowski barked, "get back to work. Don't let me see you goofing off or I'll haul your ass down to the principal's office."

In the lingo of woodshop, Hassan and I went against the grain. We both stuck out like sore thumbs— something that also happened a lot in shop because we were always accidentally hammering our thumbs instead of the head of a nail.

Mr. K retired to the back room with his clipboard to inventory wood stock. He almost always carried a clipboard with him and drew little diagrams similar to running plays of where all the wood was stacked in the storeroom.

I filed away on my paperweight, wondering what exactly a paperweight was.

On his side of the table, Kyle started singing. *Bomb, bomb, bomb. Bomb, bomb I-Rann.*

He cracked up half the class.

The song was that old Beach Boys hit, "Barbara Ann." Instead of singing the right words, Kyle made up new ones. *Bomb, bomb, bomb; Bomb, bomb I-Rann.*

The kids around him sounded like the laugh track on *Hee Haw*, a show my Granny watched like her life depended on it. She'd break your fingers if you even got near the TV knobs, if there were any.

Hassan continued sanding his paperweight.

Kyle left his work station and approached our side of the bench. He stood over Hassan. "Whatcha making there? A bomb?"

The woodshop was quiet except for the *shush-shush* of sandpaper. Everyone was looking at Hassan.

"Go away," Hassan muttered. His black bangs hung down over his eyes.

Kyle yanked Hassan's paperweight out of its vise and let it roll across the floor. "Oops."

What was taking Mr. K so long? I had just about filed my paperweight flat.

I didn't think it was any of my business what went on half a world away. Except I knew Hassan wasn't to blame. Someone should do something.

"Hey Kyle, why don't you give it a break?"

Kyle turned to me. His doughy face was splotched with freckles, so many that they seemed to puddle. "What are you going to do about it, trailer trash?"

I clenched the rasp in my hand. I told myself not to get involved. This wasn't my fight.

"Or maybe I should say *traitor* trash."

Okay, *now* it was my business.

I dropped my weapon and nailed Kyle right across

the jaw with a left hook. My fist sank into his wide, Wonder Bread face. He spun backwards. I guess toting water to the crop all summer had sprouted me some arm muscles. I had no idea I was that strong. I stood staring at my hand, knuckles throbbing.

Suddenly Mr. Koslowski grabbed me by the collar. "You're coming with me, boy, down to the principal's office."

9

Friends Stand Up
for Friends

The principal called Mama to pick me up, but Daddy had the truck and was off at a job site. So she sent Angie, who pulled up in her canary-yellow Trans Am.

"Get in," she ordered. "What the hell is wrong with you?" she yelled as she squealed out of the parking lot.

I was all the way over pressed up against the door. "I don't know."

She took one of her hands off the wheel and smacked me upside the head. "Hey!" I yelped. "Leave off."

"I'll leave off when you start talking and tell me what happened."

I wanted her to go back to driving the car instead of driving me crazy. So I ticked off one of the things that bothered me. "Kids at school call me trailer trash."

Angie rolled her eyes. "Who the hell cares?"

"I do, I guess."

She shook her head in disgust. I reported what the principal had told me. He said he wasn't going to expel me or give me a suspension. Instead, he gave me what he called a "severe warning." If I stepped out of line one more time, if he heard of one more incident, by God, I would be sent packing to Stuart so fast my head would spin. He might have said something about me being better off with my own kind. I sat in a chair opposite his desk staring down at the floor.

What did he mean, "My own kind." What were *my kind*?

A half mile later Angie started up again. "Remember when you read *Great Expectations*?"

I hesitated. I didn't trust where she was steering the conversation. Finally I let out a slow, "Yeah."

"We're reading it in my GED class."

Was this one of Angie's tricks? Talking about a book only to point out what a waste of time reading is?

She went on, "That girl, Estella, sure does have an attitude."

Takes one to know one, I thought.

"Anyway," she continued. "You never know how things are going to turn out."

I wasn't sure if she was trying to comfort me, but either way it didn't work.

I was afraid Daddy was going to let me have it. He wasn't one to use the strap, but I'd seen him mean. Angry about something not being fair. When I got home I crawled into my bunk and let the afternoon shadows climb the walls of the trailer. I strained to hear the cab door of his truck slam shut and his work boots crunch on the gravel. Mama was in the kitchen rattling cups and plates left in the dish drainer. I kicked the top bunk above me.

I hated Athens Middle School. I expected things to be different, yet it felt a lot the same. I was still the odd man out.

When Daddy came in he brought a draft of cold air and the sweet smell of unfiltered tobacco with him. He and Mama talked in hushed tones. After a minute he called me over.

"Boy."

I walked over to the couch where he sat with his feet up on the coffee table, his boots resting on top of one of Mama's magazines. Stuffing from the sofa herniated out in popcorn-size clumps.

"I'm thinking about headin' up to Columbus. I heard from a fella the other day over at the hardware store that there was a factory up there hiring."

He continued. "I'm counting on you to help your Ma and keep Granny in line."

Granny sat snoozing in her chair with the TV volume turned all the way up.

"I'll be home by Christmas just like Sant-y Claus with a big old bag of toys for the lot of ya."

Mama came and stood behind me. "Roland," she began, "I need you to be the man of the house."

Trailer, I corrected her inside my head.

"Can you do that?" Daddy asked.

"Yes, sir."

Before I turned to go hide in my bunk, he added, "Friends stand up for friends."

I watched him from my bed, watched as the blue light of the TV flickered across his spent face. My father was just as much a mystery to me as I must be to him. I think he was trying to tell me I'd done good. I just wished I knew for sure.

When I returned to school the next day I was given a wide berth walking down the hallway. Kids must've thought I was dangerous, liable to do anything. Bark or bite or foam at the mouth.

After English class, my last class of the day, Ms. Knudsen asked if she might have a word with me. Oh no, I thought.

"I heard what happened," she said. I was pretty sure it wasn't news. Word travels fast in middle school.

"Just so you know, I didn't start that fight. Kyle—"

"I'm not talking about Kyle, I'm talking about you. You sit by yourself at the last table in the cafeteria. You rush off right after school. In order to make friends, you have to be a friend."

I didn't know what to say. There seemed to be only two options as an outsider in this new middle school: being made fun of or ignored. I chose life as a loner.

"Why don't you invite someone over after school, Patty or Hassan?"

"NO!" I said, maybe a little too forcibly. I softened my tone. "No, that won't work."

"Okay, then. You don't have to."

She reached into her desk drawer. "Here, this is for you." She handed me a blue- and white-striped notebook.

"What's this?" I mean I knew what it was, but

what did she want me to do with it?

"You seem like you keep a lot bottled up inside." I nodded because I thought that was what she wanted to see.

"It's for you to record your observations, stories, whatever you want."

Was it a gift or an assignment? "Thanks a lot." I jammed the journal into my backpack, without any real intention of ever writing in it.

I emerged into the schoolyard inhaling a deep draw of fresh air. Freedom. At the edge of the blacktop was Hassan bobbling a soccer ball back and forth from foot to foot. "Kick it to me," I said. We kicked it back and forth for a few minutes until Hassan popped the ball up into the air, caught it on his knee and, after keeping that going, he headed it at me. It bounced off my chest. "Whoa, cool. How do you do that?"

He proceeded to keep the ball in the air for a full five minutes, leaning back and continuously tapping it with his foot. He was a cross between a dancer and an athlete. He passed it to me and I immediately sent it askew.

"Hey," I said, "want to see a secret hiding place?"

"Sure." Hassan ran to retrieve the ball and stuffed it into his knapsack. We took off walking down the street past fraternity houses and out towards the edge of town. Our backpacks bounced on our backs as we jogged the half-mile on the blacktop before reaching the gravel road. Instead of heading up towards the trailer, I cut a roundabout path through the woods, bushwhacking until I spotted the albino tree, stark against the gray sky. We finally arrived at the pine grove.

"This is a great hiding place," Hassan said, throwing off his backpack and sinking to the ground.

Even though it was November we were sweaty and covered with cockleburs and thistles.

"I come here when things at the trailer get too—." How would life at home sound to Hassan? "Loud." I decided it wasn't worth getting into.

"If I can remember how to get here, I will come back—when things get too—loud." He glanced over at me. "Is that all right?"

"Sure." I pulled a flattened candy bar out of my bag. I gave the less smooshed part to him. "If you think you'll need to."

"My family might have to leave."

I stopped chewing.

"My father has talked about moving." He dug around in his pack and pulled out some kind of sweet wrapped in cellophane. He broke it in two and offered me half. "He's looking for a teaching position out east."

"Back in Iran?" I took the chewy nougat candy bar covered in slivered almonds.

"No. Going back now is impossible. My uncle, the one who teaches at the university, called the other night. He said many of my parents' friends have had to go into hiding. Since the revolution there have been purges of the faculty on campus. There is as much repression now as there was under the Shah."

I scooped up a pile of dead pine needles and tried to stack them one upon the other like Lincoln logs.

"They've kicked the moderates out and the mullahs are in charge."

"What's a mullah?"

Hassan paused, thinking. "Someone who has studied the sacred scriptures. They want a government based upon the Koran. No broadcasts of rock music. Nearly all the newspapers are censored. Anything having to do with the West is being removed; no more Coca-Cola."

"Wow," I uttered in dismay.

"All over the city there is unrest. Students riot in the streets. There are firing squads in the square where people are executed."

My house of pine needles caved-in.

"I'm afraid we're stuck here for now."

I knew how that felt. "But what if you are asked

to leave the country?" President Carter had announced that all university students with invalid visas would be deported. What about Hassan and his family? Would they be forced to leave?

Hassan looked around the clearing. "Then I will run here and be safe." He bit into the chocolate. "People seem to forget, it wasn't me who took those people hostage."

"People look at me and think because I live in a trailer that I'm trash, that because I'm not a townie or my dad doesn't teach at the university that I'm not as good as they are."

Dusk was beginning to fall. What with the time change and the thick fir canopy, darkness came early. "We'd better start heading out."

When we reached the gravel road, I saw that the sky had gone all silvery, the bottom of the clouds weighted with lead.

"Can you get back?" I asked.

Hassan nodded. "Thanks."

"For what?"

Hassan cinched up his pack, fixing to jog home. "See you at school."

Of Turkey and Tehran

I was glad to sleep in on Thanksgiving Day. When I awoke the entire trailer smelled like roasted turkey and all the windows were steamed up. In my sleeping shorts I propped open the screen door to let out the heat and overpowering aroma. The sky was a bright blue and the sun had already burned off the morning frost. The cold, clear air stung my lungs and made my chest ache. But it wasn't all for the beauty or from breathing in the air.

A minor glitch. We'd been expecting Daddy, but the day before we had received in the mail a postcard with a puzzling message. In his cramped handwriting Daddy had written: *Can't come. Sory, Harland.* Stamped

CLOUD OF WITNESSES

in the upper left-hand corner was the address for the Franklin County Jail.

"Damn him," Mama said, tacking the postcard to the refrigerator door with a Burger Beer magnet. "That man's always getting himself into some kind of trouble."

"Maybe it's nothing, Mama," I tried to console her.

Mama looked at me and shook her head. "No, son, I've known your daddy for twenty-five years. It's just like him to go off and screw things up."

I turned on the TV. Football was on all the channels. Lately so much of the talk on TV had been about the crisis in Iran. One entire news show, hosted by a guy with comic-book ears named Ted Koppel, was dedicated to reporting on the hostages. After the U.S. Embassy in Iran was overrun, other Muslim countries got on the bandwagon. American embassies in Lebanon and Pakistan were also attacked. It was half-time and a Cleveland sportscaster was busy rattling off scores from other football games. In between his announcements, he took a moment to express thanks, it being Thanksgiving and all. He was proud to be an American and to live in a land of freedom. I thought back to Hassan and what he'd said at school that day. It would be hard to live in a place where people couldn't stand up for what they believed in or were afraid of being arrested for simply stating their opinions.

Then, without warning, the sportscaster set the Iranian flag on fire. "Anybody from Iran in this country who doesn't like it here," he challenged, "should leave."

Mama lumbered out into the kitchen and turned down the potatoes boiling on top of the stove. She drained them and added milk and salt and big lumps of butter for whipping. When she plugged in the electric beaters and cranked them up to high, the picture on the television set went all haywire. The flames of the Iranian flag jumped and flickered, filling the whole screen. I up and turned it off.

"Almost ready," Mama called out. "Can you make the biscuits, Roland?"

I seized the end of a tube of packaged biscuits and whacked it on the edge of the counter. It popped open like an air rifle and shot out a slab of dough. Next I arranged them on a cookie sheet and set them in the oven on a rack below the creamed corn and candied sweet potatoes. "Smells good, Mama," I said. I was looking forward to our Thanksgiving feast.

"I don't think I can eat a thing today." Granny was in one of her moods. She slumped into a chair by the kitchen table. "My stomach's been jumpy all morning. Must have been that greasy fried egg you made me for breakfast," she grumbled.

Mama ignored Granny and started pulling stuff out of the oven.

For all of Granny's whining about an upset stomach she had no trouble packing away her dinner.

Ever since her operation she was supposed to eat five or six small meals a day instead of three regular ones. So in the middle of our Thanksgiving meal Granny leaned over her coffee can.

"Please, stop that," Mama said. "The rest of us are trying to eat."

Granny belched out loud and a whiff of regurgitated cream corn wafted over the table.

"You're ruinin' my appetite." Mama bit into a turkey leg.

I had a feeling what was coming next.

"Reckless girl!" Granny bellowed. "If you hadn't of married that jailbird we'd a-been in the lap of luxury right now, living in the land of plenty."

Despite the fact that it had happened long ago, Granny had never forgiven Mama for marrying Daddy. It wasn't that she loved Mama so much she wanted to keep her all to herself. It was that Mama's marrying Daddy had interfered with her own plans.

The mines had all closed up, run out of coal, and Grandpa Jedidiah, worn out from black lung disease, had passed away. Years of working in the mines and breathing in the coal dust had eventually killed him. When the undertakers laid him out he weighed ninety-eight pounds and they say his lungs looked like they were made out of black licorice.

All her life Granny had wanted to get out of West Virginia, out of the hills, away from the mines and the company store and the whistles blowing day and night. Dee-troit or Chic-cago was where there was factory work and big money. This was her chance. She loaded up the pickup truck and piled in Bobbie Sue, Jimmy, and Ruthie (my mama), and took off on the county highway. On the first road leading north.

Ruthie was only seventeen, and as she sat in the back behind the cab with the galvanized washtub, blue- and white-striped tick mattresses, and the burlap flour sacks that held all their clothes, she sang the songs she'd learned growing up in the hills. *I'll fly away oh glory, I'll fly away.*

Mama was a country girl, through and through. She loved hearing the songbirds in the mornings, and in the evening watching the nighthawks glide easy over the hills. She loved the springtime when the rhododendron bushes bloomed scarlet and the dogwood budded white and pink.

Some glad mornin' when this life is oe'r, I'll fly away.

Often while out walking the woods, she'd pick wildflowers or healing herbs or bring home a robin's nest. Had it been up to her, she would have stayed forever in West Virginia.

Well, it wasn't up to her. As luck would have it the truck broke down right outside of Pomeroy on the Ohio side of the river. Daddy worked as a mechanic at a garage and came out with a tow truck. He looked under the hood. There wasn't much he could do for her; she was an old truck. He offered to give them a ride into town. Granny and the kids camped out behind the shop until they could figure out what to do next. Meanwhile Ruthie and Harland took to walking in the woods. Before too long there was a wedding and shortly after that Gary came along. Granny ended up staying in southern Ohio with all her big dreams of the big city rusted and stalled.

Mama pushed herself away from the table and went out to the living room.

"Don't walk away from me!" Granny picked up the turkey leg Mama had left unfinished on her plate and tossed it at Mama's back.

Mama wheeled around and hauled Granny up by her shirt collar. "Leave off or —."

Granny turned a shade of gray and passed out. Mama let go and watched her collapse back into her chair.

"Mama," I screamed, "she's dead."

"No, Roland. She's too mean to die."

I checked her breathing and listened to her heart. It was still ticking. I picked up the phone to call for an ambulance just as Granny was snapping out of it.

"Put the damn phone down," she said.

"But—"

"I ain't going to no doctor." She shifted back around to her plate and resumed eating with zeal. In between spoonfuls she threw up.

I got up, walked out the front door and followed the trail down to the ravine. If three hundred years ago the pilgrims and the Indians had gotten together and acted this way, I thought, eating and throwing up and passing out, fighting and hollering and calling each other names, then there wouldn't have been a Thanksgiving. Good thing my family didn't come over on the *Mayflower*. They'd have invented a bomb out of maize and blown each other up.

The Land of Wise Men

Come to find out Daddy's being in jail was all a mistake. He hadn't actually done anything wrong. A fellow he worked with at the Ready-Man labor agency had needed to borrow a truck for the evening and Daddy had loaned him his. What Daddy didn't know was that the guy was fixing to rob a bank. After the hold-up the police came looking for Daddy. Seems that witnesses had identified his truck as the getaway vehicle and that made him an "accessory" to the crime.

"A technicality," Daddy said, like it didn't count.

"When you getting out?" Mama asked, her voice sounding weary.

"Maybe by Christmas or until I can get all this

straightened out." Daddy said loud enough into his end of the phone so that even I could hear. But I read Mama's face. She wasn't so sure.

The first day back after Thanksgiving break, Patty invited me to stay after school in order to work on holiday decorations. I wondered if Kyle was on the decorating committee. Since our fight, I was careful not to be alone with him. I didn't want to give the principal any cause to suspend me.

When I entered the art room Hassan was already there with glitter stuck to the end of his nose. I pointed to it to help him out, but he only managed to spread the sparkles across the long bridge up to where his eyebrows met.

Patty showed us how to artfully fold a sheet of paper and then cut strategic holes so that when unfolded it looked like a crystal snowflake. Except mine kept ending up looking like bullet holes in white construction paper.

"Do you celebrate Christmas?" Patty asked Hassan, who was trying to hide his latest attempt at a snowflake.

"Christmas? No. Not really. You see the Muslim calendar is different than the Western calendar. Ours goes from full moon to full moon. So the dates shift a bit from year to year. Right now we are set to begin Muharram where we commemorate the martyrdom of Imam Hussein, the grandson of Muhammad, our prophet."

"Iman?"

"An Imam is a holy man or saint. There were only twelve Imams and the last one is said to have disappeared," he explained.

"Disappeared?" Now I was interested. What kind of wizard was this Imam?

"There was no body. He was simply taken."

Hassan picked up another sheet of paper and clipped away as if he was giving it a haircut. "The Imam Hussein and his family were killed marching across the desert. His enemies didn't believe Hussein was the rightful heir to carry on Muhammad's message and so he was assassinated by his rivals. Beheaded."

"Cool," I murmured while Patty gasped.

"How about presents? Do you give gifts?" Patty attempted to reinforce one of my snowflakes with scotch tape.

"No gifts are given. Instead there are reenactments of the Imam's death, or *ta'ziyeh* plays as they are called."

I imagined a well-lit church with the stage all set. Camels and donkeys, men dressed as shepherds parade in, and then, instead of a nativity, a massacre.

"But, the Shah outlawed the *ta'ziyeh*. The people had to perform them in secret."

"Why?" I asked. I could see why people didn't like him and were glad to see him go.

"Because the Shah was constantly afraid—what's the word—paranoid, that the people might gather and conspire to assassinate him."

Hassan went on, "The Wise Men of your Christmas story were from Persia which is now Iran."

I thought about that. Funny how the past gets tangled up in the least suspecting ways. People and their stories are more the same than different. Papery white flakes piled up on the table before us.

Patty changed the subject. "Don't be surprised after the first of the year when Ms. Knudsen asks you guys if you want to be part of the *Whiz Kidz*."

"I'm not so sure that's something I want to do," I blustered.

"Why?" Patty asked, astonished. "You're like at the head of the class in English."

It was my turn to be surprised. "I am?"

Patty rolled her eyes. "Anyway," she went on, "there's a chance for prizes and to win a college scholarship."

"College?"

Even though I lived in a college town, the idea of *going* to college seemed remote. None of my family had gone to OU except to clean the dorms (that was Mama, until her car died—or was killed by Larry). Suddenly *Whiz Kidz* had a certain appeal. Especially if I could beat out Kyle for a spot. "Do you think I have a chance?" I asked.

"You and Hassan both." Patty leaned back to observe her work. She'd been hooking fishing line through the snowflakes so that when strung up it looked like they were falling right from the ceiling tiles. "You're strong in English and Literature. Hassan can have Math."

He beamed. Or should I say, sparkled.

"I'll do Biology and Earth Science. Kyle is *very* good in world affairs and politics."

At the mention of his name I lopped off an important part of a fledgling snowflake, making it look more like an egg. "Really?" I muttered.

"His family has lived all over. In fact last week he told me about his dad being kidnapped while in Beirut a few years ago."

So do Patty and Kyle talk together a lot? I wondered.

"Groups do that," Hassan began. "It's one way to get money for their cause, taking businessmen or—"

"Embassy workers," I interjected, and then immediately felt bad.

Hassan stopped chopping. "I thought by now that the hostages would be released."

Negotiations for the embassy hostages had bogged down. As soon as President Carter or one of his envoys cleared a hurdle, the Ayatollah would make another demand. It probably didn't help that angry street mobs kept burning dummy puppets of the president. The latest development was that U.S. ships were patrolling the gulf to make sure Iranian oil was not exported. An embargo, they called it. The Ayatollah Khomeini came out with a statement saying he would sink the U.S. Navy in blood.

"Whatever," Patty continued. "His father was returned and immediately left Lebanon. He teaches Political Science at OU."

Well that explained why Kyle seemed to be so trigger-happy when it came to the hostage crisis.

Patty reached over and took my scissors. I'd been trying to even out my egg snowflake and with each snip I was only making it smaller and smaller. "Let me help," she said, politely.

The touch of her hand on mine sent shivers down my spine. Which had nothing to do with being cold or snowflakes or frosted snowmen, but more with how beautiful she was. She could give all my snowflakes a makeover if she wanted to, as long as she let me hold her hand.

95

I had nothing to compare this feeling to, the tightening in my chest—or was it my heart? All those love poems out there in the world—where did they get the words, because I had none. The only thing that might come close was the excitement I felt when Daddy and I were called into the superintendent's office and I thought, *Here's my chance.*

Patty resumed cutting and I went back to folding, the only thing I seemed good at.

It Came Upon a
Midnight Clear

"Watch out now, Granny."

I had a sheet of wrapping paper spread across the living room floor. It was Christmas Eve and I was busy wrapping a present for Mama.

Our trailer was decorated with homely ornaments, either handmade or bought cheap at the dime store. Mama had tried to spruce the place up by hanging garlands of evergreens and sprigs of holly berries around the room. Draped across the front windows was a strand of colored lights, of which about half worked. When the bulbs got really hot they blinked off and on, and I had to quick unplug them before they blew a fuse. In a corner on top of my plywood desk was a little plastic Nativity scene. It, too, had seen better days. The tiny heads of Mary and Joseph had snapped off. Their decapitated bodies leaned lovingly over a trough holding a glitter-strewn Jesus. Often at night beneath the soft glow of the colored lights, I'd gaze inside the barn, a lowly place, at the babe in the manger.

If Jesus could be born in the wrong place, why not me?

Granny tramped across my wrapping paper and heaved herself into her old vinyl chair. "Whatcha wrapping up there?" she asked.

"It's a paperweight," I said, taping up the four holes Granny's cane had left on the paper.

My answer didn't shed any more light on the subject than if I'd said it was the by-product of nuclear fusion. Granny leaned over and gingerly picked up the lopsided wooden paperweight as if it were fragile. I couldn't tell if she was impressed or perplexed by it.

She handed it back to me. "I got her a gift, too, the other day when I was up at the Woolworth store in town." She pulled a wad of toilet paper out of her housecoat pocket and handed it to me. "Wrap that up for me, honey, will ya?"

"Sure, Granny. What is it?" I undid the folds to find nestled in the tissue a small ruby-red glass bird. I held it up to the light and looked through it. "This is right pretty, Granny."

"Yeah, I thought she could put it in that raggedy bird's nest of hers she sets so much store by."

While Granny slept in her chair, I wrapped up the few presents I had managed to make or pick up here and there. I had the TV turned on low lest I awake her. Every once in a while she'd twitch, involuntarily flinging her hands in the air, only to settle back into loud snoring. The evening news was on. *"This is one of the holiest days of the Iranian year,"* the announcer said, *"marking the end of the first ten days of the holy month called Muharram."*

A throng of men and boys wearing black shirts marched across the screen. As they walked they swung a chain back and forth across their shoulders to the rhythm of beating drums. Women robed from head to foot lined the street crying and moaning. They seemed to tremble as if in a frenzy. As the camera zoomed in, I saw that the black shirts of the men and boys were stained crimson from the razor-tipped whips they used to beat their backs. *"The distinct salty smell of blood mixed with the scent of rosewater sprinkled from the crowd permeates the air,"* observed the reporter.

A sudden banging and scuffling outside our screen door startled me. Angie burst in with an armload of stuff that didn't look like presents. "Where's Mama?" she demanded.

"Merry Christmas to you, too," I said.

"Here I am, baby." Mama shuffled out of her bedroom with her hair standing straight up like she'd been napping. "What's going on?"

"I've left him, Mama. I swear to God I've left him for good." Angie left her husband Bill about every other month. Angie and Bill lived in town, off of Court Street, above Pony's Pizza where Bill worked delivering pizzas and just down the street from where Angie cut hair.

Mama heated up a cup of coffee for Angie and sat down at the kitchen table with her. Angie immediately began to wail. "He never listens to me, Mama. He don't love me no more."

"Who can blame him?" I muttered under my breath as Angie carried on.

"Roland," Mama interrupted Angie, "go out to your sister's car and help bring in her stuff, will ya."

Later that night Angie was still running off at the mouth and Granny was in one of her moods. "For heaven's sake what is that smell?" she bellowed from the depths of her chair. "Someone fart and set it on fire?"

"Angie's giving Mama a pedicure," I said.

"A *what?*" The pitch to Granny's voice was an octave above normal.

"Painting her toenails," I explained.

"Oh, for Pete's sake. Cut it out, you're making me sick."

I grudgingly got up and fetched Granny her coffee can from under the kitchen table. Chalk this up, I thought, another ruined holiday. "Tell us a story, Mama," I begged, hoping the distraction might do us all some good.

Angie leaned over Mama's big toe with her teeny, tiny brush. "Yeah, Mama." It must be a Christmas miracle—Angie agreeing with me on something. "Tell us one from when you were a girl."

Granny made gagging sounds like she was going to throw up.

Mama examined Angie's handiwork by holding her foot up to the kitchen light. "This looks right pretty. Thank you, baby girl. Well, I don't know if I got any stories to tell."

"A Christmas story," I suggested.

Mama thought a minute. "There was this thing that happened. Ain't sure if it's true or not, but it still makes for a good story.

"Go ahead," Angie and I urged.

"I reckon I was about eight years old that

Christmas. The snow was falling like feathers out of a pillow. We could barely make out the lights down below in town where the mines were open all night long. The men who ran the mines were tight-fisted. They rarely took into account holidays and time off. The owners figured they had to give the miners Christmas, but they weren't about to let them have Christmas Eve, too.

"My daddy's shift had ended at about noon and the last shift of the day was still down in the mines as midnight came on. It was getting to be about quitting time and I'm sure each man was thinking about his family and spending Christmas with them. Maybe they had already bought a piece of candy, a spinning top, or even a doll on credit from the company store. A doll was a big present for those days."

Mama looked in Granny's direction, but Granny shifted her body toward the wall.

"They were just fixing to come up from below when the mine caved in. The horn in town blew, which meant that there was trouble in the mines. People poured out of their houses. It was the worst sound a woman could hear, thinking that her man might be trapped hundreds of feet below the ground. There wasn't a single family in town that hadn't lost a loved one down in those mines."

The wind outside had picked up and was rattling

a loose piece of aluminum siding on the trailer.

"Me and my brothers and sisters came outside all bundled up in our sweaters and jackets to have a look. Like I said, the snow was coming down hard. A layer of coal dust darkened the snow around the elevator leading down to the mineshaft. Women stood around the opening. Some of them cried into their hands and shawls. No one wanted to scare us children, but we already knew the truth. Those men might not get out.

"A rescue crew came in and asked us to back off. I was cold and hungry anyway. Mama and Daddy took us home to lie down and wait for morning.

"That morning, long ago, I remember waking up and thinking something big had happened. I thought and recollected it was Christmas. Yonder by the window on my little wooden chair that Daddy had made me was a doll. She had beautiful golden hair and little painted-on red cheeks. When I tipped her over she mewed just like a wee kitten. I jumped for joy."

Granny craned her neck around to give Mama the evil eye.

"Mama gave me a look that quieted me right down. I pulled on my coat and ran down the hill to the mineshaft to see if there was any news.

"They were just beginning to report that they might have found something. There was a rumble of hope throughout the crowd. One of the rescue crew thought he heard a man calling beyond a wall of rock down in the hole. Everyone got excited. I whooped and danced around because it was Christmas, and because my toes were cold."

I tried to imagine Mama as a skinny little girl, with her hair going ever which way. "A little later they pulled a man up out of the mine hole. He was covered from head to toe with coal soot. The only thing you could make out was the whites of his eyes and his teeth, and even then he didn't have many of those. His wife and kids clung to him and cried. He pushed them off and spoke to the crowd.

"'I saw him,' he said to all around him.

"'Who?' the women asked, each one hoping for word of her man.

"'I seen the Christ child asleep in his little manger.'

"No one said a word. I wasn't sure at all what the miner was talking about.

"'After the walls came down we all thought we was goners. I couldn't see nothing. It was pitch black. Not even my hand in front of my face. I prayed to God to help me. I prayed all night long. I never heard nothing but a few groans from the others'n down there with me, and after a while that stopped too.'

So they were all dead except for this man.

"The man went on, talking excitedly. 'I musta fell off and slept some 'cause I was awoke by a light at the other end of the tunnel. I crawled down to it and there crouched next to a coal seam was a baby boy all wrapped up in rags.'

"I felt sorry for the man and his family. He must have lost his mind down in the darkness for so long. They were fixing to carry him off to the hospital in Wheeling about two hours away. The whole time he kept saying over and over again, 'I seen it. I seen the Christ child.'"

The colored Christmas lights in the room began to blink. Green, blue, yellow, red. I jumped up to shut them off, but before I could get to them there was a sound outside. I was a bit spooked after hearing Mama's story, afraid it might be the mad miner come back to us.

"Angie! Angie, com'on outta here, now."

I peeked through the curtains. Sure enough, it was a crazy man—Angie's husband Bill. He was outside in the snow calling for her. Bright moonlight lit up his long Lynyrd Skynyrd hair.

Angie whipped open the screen door and hollered back, "Make me, you son of a bitch."

"Baby, I'm a sorry about ever thang." He had a rough voice smoothed over by one too many beers.

"Don't make no difference. We're through." Angie

slammed the door shut. The whole trailer shook.

"Something smells bad." Granny bellyached.

I sniffed the air. I smelled it too. It smelled like—spilled nail polish and grilled evergreen garlands.

I looked up just in time to see the Christmas lights sputter and spark, catching the living room curtains on fire. Flames began to consume the flimsy fabric. Within seconds the front room was full of putrid yellow smoke.

"Fire!" yelled Angie, rushing for the front door. She jumped into Bill's arms.

I grabbed Granny and hauled her out. "Put me down," she yipped, beating me on the back. "Put me down, I say." I plopped her into a snowdrift.

"Where's Mama?" I managed to ask while leaning over, hacking and spitting to clear my lungs.

Without waiting for an answer, I ran back in. "Mama," I screamed, "where're you at?"

Mama appeared like a ghost right in front of me. "Right here. I just needed to get my old doll and bird's nest. These are my treasures. I didn't want 'em to burn up." I shoved Mama through the open screen door and out into the yard.

Before going out the door I reached up and yanked on the curtains, or what was left of them.

Whuff! The material not yet completely engulfed plus the rod came crashing down. I stomped on the burning cinders with my stocking feet, scorching the pads of my feet, just like Pip in *Great Expectations* battling the blaze in Miss Havisham's decaying bridal suite. Carefully, using the curtain rod as a poker, I lifted the smoldering strand of hot lights and tossed them out into the snow where they sizzled like meat on a spit for a few seconds.

Angie and Bill by this time had made up with each other and were rolling around in the snow kissing and hugging. "Baby, baby," he kept saying over and over. "What would I'a done without cha?"

Granny, her bare legs under her housecoat all askew and red from the cold, croaked at me. "Get me out of here, dang it. Roland, if I get my hands on you . . . I'm . . . I'm gonna kill you."

Mama danced around in her bare feet, clutching her old doll baby to her chest. She probably looked just as she had when she was a little girl, skipping and bouncing in the cold, happy to be alive and, most likely, because her feet were freezing. Her toes with the red-painted toenails were turning blue. "Let's get on back inside and see what we can clean up," she said.

The whole house stank like scorched synthetics. We opened the windows, their glass panes blackened, to let in fresh air. Bill threw the rest of the singed curtains outside with the dead Christmas lights. The outlet the lights had been plugged into was charred and the plastic cover had melted. The veneer on the fake paneling around the doorframe had bubbled up and peeled back. Granny dusted off her vinyl chair and sat down.

A gust of gray ash whooshed out from between her legs.

Mama toted her treasures back to their shelf in her room.

There wasn't much for me to do but put on clean socks and salve my feet. I retreated to my bunk bed off the living room. A cool cross-breeze between the open windows and door blew over me. Mingled with the clean scent of new-fallen snow was the aroma of wet smoke. Angie and Bill slow danced to Christmas music coming from her portable transistor radio.

Sometime in the middle of the night, I awoke, my feet bothering me. Angie and Bill were asleep on the foldout couch. I lay there listening to the seesaw rhythm of their breathing, and something else—words on the wind blowing across the hills. In my dreams I saw a crazy man with long hair beating his back bloody and raw, crying out over and over again, "I seen the Christ child, I seen 'im."

13

Nomads Looking for a Home

Chances for a peaceful new year and new decade in 1980 were slim. After Russia invaded Afghanistan there was talk of a third world war, a war of the worlds, a regular nuclear blow-out between the Soviet Union, China, the Middle East, and America. At the same time the hostage crisis in Iran dragged on and on.

Daddy had gotten himself a free lawyer assigned by the courts. The judge found it hard to dismiss his case outright because of his police record. His trial date was set for the middle of April. Other than that he said he couldn't gripe—three square meals a day—except that a cold had settled in his chest and he had to sleep sitting up at night in order to breathe properly.

In English class at school we were studying Shakespeare. One wintry day, school had been canceled because an inch and a half of snow had fallen overnight and the school buses couldn't get back into the hills to pick up the country kids. If a bus had to back up, it might slide off the road and end up in a gully. I was sitting at home on the register where the heat comes out, trying to stay warm while reading *The Merchant of Venice*. I had just read, "In sooth, I know not why I am so sad," when I heard a *pop pop* sound. I stood up in time to see a grey car gunning up and down the hills the bus drivers were too afraid to drive on. As the car drew closer I saw it wasn't actually gray—that was just the color of all the duct tape holding it together. The little Datsun pulled into the drive and before stalling out it backfired like to raise the dead or wake up Granny. Larry unfolded himself from behind the steering wheel. He waved to me as if he'd been gone for a lifetime instead of three months.

"Howdy there, little buddy," Larry said, thrusting a grocery sack stuffed with tacky carnival castoffs into my arms. "Happy Birthday."

"You're a little late, Larry. My birthday was last month. I'm fourteen now." I helped tote stuff in. "Where's the Impala?"

Granny was asleep in her vinyl chair while Mama

eased herself up off the couch where she'd been watching her soap operas. "Well, ain't this a surprise," she said, giving Larry a hug that took the wind out of him.

"I got presents for y'all." He reached for the bag I was holding and dug around in it. "You still like the Oak Ridge Boys, Mama?"

"You know I do."

Larry handed Mama a glass mirror with a picture of the Oak Ridge Boys with last year's date decaled onto it. She held the flimsy souvenir in her hands and admired it as if it were an antique.

"And for Roland here I've got a real classic." He presented me with a Coke bottle that had been heated up then stretched and twisted into an S shape. "You can actually drink out of it, but you'll need a crooked straw." Larry ribbed me as if he'd told a funny joke.

"Whatcha got there for me?" Granny sat up, fully awake.

"This pig," he said, tossing a stuffed pink pig with a black snout in her direction. Granny let it fall to the ground beside her chair.

"I thought you was goin' to be gone all winter," Mama said, making room for Larry on the couch.

"I wish," Granny muttered.

"Well, things are sort of slow right now. I was down in Myrtle Beach working at a brand-new putt-putt golf course." He whistled. "A regular work of art, that place. They got two courses—one a tropical jungle theme where you can hit a hole-in-one right through King Kong's mouth. The other side is Chinese Palaces where one of the hazards is a samurai sword guy that'll chop your ball in half if'n you ain't careful."

He paused and looked around the room at the blistered and blackened walls, at the naked windows without curtains, at the scorched carpeting near the door. "So what's new?"

Larry brought home just enough money to help Mama stock up on groceries and pay the electric bill. After that was spent, Bill got him a job at Pony's Pizza helping to deliver pizzas. Larry reckoned he'd stay until the snow melted before moving on.

Of all the holidays celebrated at school, I hated Valentine's Day the most. While at Stuart Elementary I had despised the giving and receiving of penny valentines, but Athens Middle School went one step further by planning a dance. At lunchtime Patty singled me out.

"You're coming, aren't you?" she asked.

My little paper valentine heart spouted "XXXOOO" in starry bubbles like the kind you see over cartoon character's heads. Was she actually inviting me to the dance? "Sure," I managed to squeak out.

"I mean," and she paused to smile, her teeth lining up evenly like houses in a subdivision, "to help with the decorations."

"Sure," I repeated, bringing my voice down a notch.

During sixth period study hall Hassan and I walked over to the gym.

"Great, you're here!" Patty seemed genuinely happy to see us.

Whenever I was around Patty I felt nervous, like riding in a car with Larry. I never knew what was around the next corner.

"We need someone to cut out a gazillion hearts." She pointed to a long table with pink and red construction paper scattered across the surface. Then she turned toward me. "Roland, can you help me put up these streamers?"

I held a ladder for Patty while Hassan took a seat at the table and began cutting. Before climbing up she took off her shoes and socks. She wore peg leg jeans that tapered down to her thin ankles. I noticed her second toe was much longer than her big toe, thin and cylindrical almost like a finger digit. Her toes gripped the slat steps. My eyes were fixed on the knob where her anklebone stuck out. It was the most glorious thing

I'd ever seen—creamy white with a tiny freckle in the center. Something surged inside of me, like a meteor in my blood.

As she stretched upward to drape a braid of streamers over the basketball hoop, I reached out and touched her ankle-knob.

Patty shrieked and lost her balance. I caught her in my arms.

"Whoa!" She looked up at me. Her eyes were blue—not slate blue like mine, but a light blue like the winter sky or like—. "You can put me down now," she said shyly.

"Oh. Sorry."

Patty straightened her shirt, which had bunched up. "S'okay." We both stared at each other for a second and then cast our eyes away self-consciously.

"How you doing there, Hassan?" I asked, feeling the need for man-to-man interaction.

He held up a pink blob shaped like the stump of the headless chicken at the freak show.

"What is it?" Patty and I asked together.

"Well, the human heart isn't exactly like this," he said, referring to the valentine heart template in front of him. "It's more like this with the aorta valves and the right and left ventricle and the right and left atrium and—."

Patty rolled her eyes. I whispered to Hassan, "Just do it how people expect it, man. No one really cares."

The gym that afternoon was packed. Kids lined the walls and bleachers. A rock band from the local high school played Kiss and The Who songs until Ms. Knudsen told them to go for something a little more conventional. They switched gears and did an up-tempo number called "Afternoon Delight." Hassan and I stood off to the side selling brownies, cookies, and cupcakes made by the PTA committee.

We're going to slow things down a bit," said the long-haired vocalist into the microphone. "Give you guys a chance to get close." The principal standing beneath the scoreboard broadcast a forbidding look. "Uh, well, not too close. You know."

A handful of brave couples gathered on the hardwood floor to slow dance. They clung to each other as they shuffled their feet. It looked like they were basically holding one another up. I looked over at Patty serving punch at the next table. She had her hair loosely pulled back into a ponytail. Tendrils of escaped hair fell down into her eyes that she had to tuck behind her ears. She looked up and smiled at me from across the room.

"She's great," Hassan said.

"Uhmm," I answered in blissful agreement.

Patty stepped out from behind her table. My heart jumped in panic. If she asked me to dance, I was going to have to tell her I didn't know how. Even the slow stuff where they were barely moving would mean getting out in front of people.

"This is boring!" Patty exclaimed.

"What is this?" Hassan was referring to the kids moving as if in slow motion before us. "This is *not* dancing."

We watched as the few couples gave up and went to sit on the bleachers. I also saw Kyle sitting off by himself on a bench. For a fraction of a second I felt sorry for him, but then thought, *nah*, and turned my attention to Patty.

"This is a disaster," Patty declared.

She was right. I could have told her a Valentine's Day dance wouldn't work.

"Follow me guys."

Patty went out to the basketball court and stood right on the silly Bobcat-mascot face in the middle.

Hassan and I looked at each other. I had no idea what she was planning.

She began to move her arms, as if she were flapping, like a gangly bird. I'd watched an episode of *Solid Gold* on TV, so I knew a little about dance. What Patty was doing was a combination of running in place, arhythmic jumping, aerobics, and charades thrown in. Even the musicians didn't know what to do when Patty lunged on one knee. The bass guitarist hit a note. She thrashed about like a drunken robot. A few kids around me snickered nervously.

"We've got to do something," Hassan whispered.

"I know, but what?" There was no way I was going to enter the center of the gladiator arena to be torn apart by curious eyes.

"We can't leave her out there all alone."

What did he mean *we*?

Ms. Knudsen had moved around the court perimeter and was behind me. "Oh man, so cool."

Patty motioned for Kyle to join her.

I knew that wasn't going to happen. A kid came up and I went back to the table to wait on him. He took his time, studying each cookie. When I looked back up, Hassan was gone. He was out on the dance floor spinning around like a yo-yo on a string. Stopping for a dizzy second, he fell into her. Kyle was on his feet. I thought he was going to run out and punch Hassan. Patty just laughed and continued bouncing.

I heard someone say she was doing the Pogo.

Which made sense, sort of. The kid in front of me selected five cookies. Slowly he counted out the correct change. Then I heard a cheer.

Kyle had joined them. For a big guy he was shaking some grooves. Seems that running tackle was paying off.

It was as if the rock band woke up. The guitarist waved his arms and strummed so fast and hard that I thought he was going to break the strings, as if he was trying to get inside his guitar. The drummer was going crazy standing up and wailing on the drum skin with his sticks. The small gym sounded like it might explode from the concussive, chaotic beat.

Other kids stepped out. Bopping and bumping. They became one throbbing movement, akin to a heart pumping. I lost sight of Patty, Hassan, and Kyle in the fray. I watched a couple who had been slow dancing earlier chase each other around the gym. Someone knocked into the punch table and the contents of the bowl sloshed, creating a red lake on the wood floor. I abandoned my post and waded into the middle. The crowd closed behind me as I jostled my way inside until I was finally standing next to Patty. The temperature at the core was volcanic. Patty glistened with sweat. I got carried away by her shiny face—or maybe I was being moved along by the crowd. I grabbed her hand, hoping to find an anchor. Instead she slammed into me.

God, it was great! Who would have guessed that dancing was a contact sport!

Eventually the sidelined teachers sprang into action in an attempt to bring order. Mr. Koslowski slipped on the punch-slick floor and ended up grabbing my homeroom teacher, Miss Red-Squirrel, bringing them both down on top of each other. At some point Ms. Knudsen went over and pulled the plug on the band while Mr. K from a prone position blew his whistle.

Game over.

Hassan and I stayed late to help the custodian sweep and mop up the mess made by the mayhem. Kyle contributed by pushing the retractable bleachers back against the walls. Patty offered us the leftover cookies that didn't sell. A plate heaped with broken hearts.

"No, thanks," I said, but Hassan stuffed them into his pocket.

The school building, emptied of rowdy students, had a hollow feel; the random locker opening and closing echoed off the hallway walls. One by one the fluorescent lights were extinguished, leaving a fuzzy silence in their wake.

Hassan, Kyle, Patty and I, none of us knew quite how to say goodbye. We were all revved up from the action, a motor unable to stop. Together we walked across the school grounds toward Court Street. The afternoon was descending into twilight. I sort of wished it wasn't so late, so I wouldn't have to go home. Ice crystals twinkled around the street lamps just flashing on.

All of a sudden I spotted a gray duct-taped Datsun cruising down the street. Within a second it had pulled up next to us. "Hey, y'all. Need a ride?" Larry called out through his open window.

"No," I said, trying to quickly get rid of him.

"Who are you?" Kyle asked.

"It's the guy from the carnival." Hassan's uni-brow zigzagged as if not sure what was happening.

Larry flung open the passenger door. "Com'on— it's cold enough to freeze your balls off."

My better instincts told me this wasn't such a great idea, but I got into the passenger seat anyway. "This is my brother."

"Why didn't you say so," Kyle said, climbing into the back and taking up most of the bench seat. It was a tight squeeze, but Hassan slipped in beside him, and Patty, seeing no alternative, perched herself on Kyle's lap. He didn't seem to mind.

Larry immediately gave the car some gas. Patty squealed and Kyle grabbed her to keep her from falling. She relaxed into him.

"Whatcha y'all been doin'?" Larry asked, his head turned toward the backseat.

"Hey, Larry!" I squawked as the car bounced off a curb. "Keep your eyes on the road."

"We were at a school dance," Patty said, looking very comfortable in Kyle's arms.

"Y'all mixing it up a little bit? Huh? A little hanky-panky?" He winked at me sitting next to him in the front seat.

"Hanky-panky?" Hassan repeated.

"He means making out," Patty translated.

"Turn around," I said firmly. "and let us off at the doughnut shop. We'll take it from there."

"No can do. I got to get this pizza delivered. Our motto is thirty minutes or free. Boss'll have my ass if I don't get this pizza there in time." Larry speeded up.

Hassan looked around. "I've never been in a car like this before."

"It's not a car," I said, "it's a death trap."

About a mile outside of town, heading toward The Plains, we hit a patch of ice.

"Hold on," Larry whooped as he pumped the brake and tried to regain control of the vehicle.

The Datsun fishtailed. Patty, Hassan, and Kyle screamed while I grabbed for the little handle right above the door—the one Larry referred to as the "ohmygod" handle.

We slid on the roadway for what seemed an eternal second before falling over the edge and into a ditch.

After a moment of stunned silence, where the only thing moving was the windshield wipers swishing back and forth, Patty stated the obvious. "We've had an accident."

"Damn," Larry moaned, "the pizza. There goes my job."

"Is everyone all right?" I asked, a little wobbly.

"My reflex was to try to stop the car, but I didn't have a brake," Hassan answered.

Kyle and Patty were still clutching each other.

Larry got out to check for damages and to clear the tailpipe of snow. Little rivers of snow and ice flowed down off the windows. Larry got back in. "There is no tailpipe. We musta lost her."

"Is that it?" Hassan pointed down the road to a metal object with frayed duct-tape blowing in the wind.

"No," Larry said, "that's the bumper."

I rubbed my temples in an effort to clear away the cobwebs and the creeping cold coming in through the rusted-out floorboards. "We've got to get out of here."

Larry opened the pizza box. Steam wafted into his face. "It's still hot." He smacked his lips. "Hand me a beer, will ya. It's in the ice chest on the floor back there."

Kyle searched around his feet.

"You kids want somethin' to eat?"

Patty shook her head. "Roland's right. I've got to get home. My mom and dad will be worried. I'm game to walk, how about you guys?"

Hassan, Kyle, and I erupted in unison. "Yes!"

We left Larry washing pizza back with beer.

A couple cars passed us, but after a while nothing. All around us the snow seemed to emit an inner glow as if stored away in each of those individual flakes was radioactive material.

"I love walking in the snow," Patty said. She had a pointy stocking cap that was about seven feet long. She wrapped the end around her neck like a scarf.

"I do, too," Hassan chimed in. "Back home I could see the peak of Mount Damavand from our rooftop terrace. During the winter my family would take skiing holidays up to the mountains."

We walked close to the side of the road, darkness hovering around us.

"I love to ski!" Patty said. "I haven't been anywhere great like Iran. Just local resorts up around Bellefontaine."

"You must've been rich," I put in.

"No, not really," Hassan said. "It was easy to get

to the mountains and fairly inexpensive to rent skis.

I couldn't imagine my family skiing. "I'm freezing." I blew into my bare hands and then jammed them deep inside my coat pockets. "Wish I'd worn a hat and gloves."

"Here." Kyle offered his hat. "My coat has a hood."

"I'm warm enough for the time being," Patty said. "Take my gloves."

Hassan pulled the cookies out of his pocket. "Would anyone care for a broken heart?"

Patty looked at the pieces. "Now that actually looks like a human heart. There's the left ventricle and the—" Hassan tossed some crumbs at Patty. "Hey!" She laughed.

I could imagine my family skiing. Larry aiming right for a tree and Mama with her hair every which way stopping halfway down to observe a snow hare, or Granny cackling and hooting sledding down, with Jedidiah steering. Only Daddy would think it was all for naught and stand under the eaves of the hot chocolate hut with a coffee and cigarette. Cold air hurts his lungs.

Patty threw snow at Hassan, who ducked. Hassan made a snowball and hurled it at her.

"Come fight on my side," Patty called out to me.

"You want your gloves back?" I asked her.

She screamed. Kyle grabbed her by the waist and

flung her onto a soft mound. "Dogpile," he shouted. Hassan stood and gawked, having no idea what a dogpile is.

I could never be like them, playing around. I could never be like anybody. I was too damn cold. "Com'on, y'all. We've got miles to cover."

In the distance I spied a cozy house; it looked so warm and inviting. If I lived there I'd be home already, I thought. Perhaps I'd been switched at birth and my real parents worked at the university and took ski holidays.

Patty, Hassan, and Kyle stopped goofing around and we continued walking.

"Tell us something warm about Iran," Patty implored Hassan.

He thought for a minute. "Often my family would take automobile rides out into the country, driving past fields of ripe melons."

"Mmm, I love watermelons," Patty said dreamily.

"My father would stop and cut one off the vine. The sweetest I've ever tasted."

My mouth watered.

"We'd picnic in the hills. One time we went to pay homage at the mosque in the holy city of Isfahan. I remember walking down the Chahar Bagh, a type of boulevard lined with date palm trees and magnificent gardens, past the pavilions and palaces and the polo fields where the kings used to play. The blue tiles of the mosque seemed to borrow their color from the blue sky. It was—" He stopped and sighed. "It was so beautiful."

I detected a note of sadness in Hassan's voice. "Tell us something hot about Iran," I said.

"We have two famous deserts, the *Dasht-i Kavir* and the *Dasht-i Lut*. *Dasht-i Lut* was named after Lot, the nephew of Abraham. The area was contaminated by evil men and judged by God. Now it is a salt desert. Beneath the crust of salt run underground rivers of quicksand. Many a trader, especially in older days, was accidentally sucked under, him and his camel."

"Cool!" Kyle exclaimed.

"Gross!" Patty shivered.

"Windstorms can come up quickly and blind a caravan crossing the desert."

Dry snow blew across the county road before us. I felt like a nomad in an arctic desert.

Suddenly a pair of headlights flared behind us. We waved frantically for the car to stop. It slowed down and pulled off the shoulder. Out popped Larry from the passenger seat. "See, I got y'all a ride." He grinned from ear to ear.

Hassan, Kyle, and Patty cheered.

We squished in. The driver hesitated for a moment. Larry wasn't in the car.

"Where's Larry?" I asked.

About ten feet from the open passenger-side door was Larry relieving himself. A steady stream of steam rose up from the snow. I wished right then and there to be sucked down by the undertow of quicksand.

Larry jumped back into the car and instructed the driver.

"Let her rip."

Clowns of Witnesses

After the snow melted Larry left to meet up with the other carnies working their way north. Before leaving, he stripped the Datsun of parts and pushed the duct-taped chassis down the hill toward the ravine. He got what he could for the engine and tires and gave the money to Mama. It wasn't much.

I was hungry—not for the canned peas and oatmeal Mama picked up at the food bank. I craved something new, fresh, exciting. I'd look out over the barren brown hills and dream of green—a carpet of clover, tender young shoots, waxy buds. But nothing came of my hankering. Daddy was still locked up, and so too the hostages, and at school we were studying the Civil War, caught up in a conflict that four years of bloody war still hadn't seemed to settle.

Some might call it cabin fever, a yearning for spring or some unnamable longing. To quote Shakespeare: "In sooth, I know not why I am so sad." Each morning I woke up, only to sleepwalk through the day.

"Roland, time to get up. Oatmeal's on the table."

One afternoon I came home from school to find Granny dancing a jig with her four-legged cane. I was curious and terrified at the same time. "What's going on?"

Granny held out a flier she had picked up at the county medical office where she got her codeine. "There's to be a revival," she announced, "and we're a-goin'. Call your sister up and tell her to get her butt over here."

For someone with a teeny, tiny heart who begrudged every favor asked of her, Angie was already working at top capacity. As it was, she drove out to the trailer three times a week to drop off "mistake" pizzas and chauffeur Mama and Granny everywhere. I wasn't sure how this new request was going to go over.

"Hello, Angie, Granny was wondering if you'd take her up to a church meeting?"

"Tell her to go to hell," was Angie's reply.

Granny came out of her bedroom wearing

makeup. Her lipstick looked like she'd applied it with a paint roller.

"Now, Angie," I said, trying to charm her. Things would not go well in the trailer if Granny didn't get her way.

"Tell her I need a goddamn blessing." Granny's charcoaled eyebrows hung crooked over her glaring eyes. She reminded me of the Ayatollah Khomeini.

"Angie, she ain't gonna take no for an answer. She has her heart set. Do it this once, please," I pleaded.

"Okay," she relented, "just this once, and after this the old witch can take her broomstick to church."

"Tell her to wear a dress," Granny added right before I hung up the phone.

Angie skidded into the gravel parking lot of the Stuart Creek Holiness Church in her '68 Trans Am. I agreed to go along to the revival meeting. I told Mama it was to help keep Granny in line, but deep down inside I wanted a blessing too. Something good, like great expectations.

On the sign board out front of the old clapboard church were the posted times for Holy Ghost Revival Week: prayer from six to seven p.m., services began at seven with no mention of when they ended. The guest speaker was Gertie Haywood.

I turned to Granny and scowled at her. "What's this about?"

I remembered Gertie was her first love. It seemed that Granny was interested in reviving not only her soul, but also an old flame.

"Well, I might do a little fishing of men, reel in old Gertie Haywood," she said, with a twinkle in her faded eyes.

"I thought he was married."

"He's a widow-man."

I shook my head. "But, Granny, it's been years. Why would Gertie Haywood be interested in you now?"

Granny checked her reflection in the rearview mirror. She patted down her flyaway gray hair. "What? You think he wouldn't want to marry me? I'll have you know I was the prettiest girl that side of the mountain—"

"Then why'd he run off with Wanda Puck?" Angie interrupted.

Granny shot Angie the evil eye. It was then that I knew I was in for a hell of an evening.

I slumped down in a metal fold-out seat in the back of the hall. The service opened with a round of choruses sung over and over in high-pitched monotone voices. *"Some glad morn' when this life is o'er, I'll fly away, To a land on God's celestial shore, I'll fly away."*

Granny banged her tambourine and winked at Gertie Haywood as he walked down the aisle on his way to the stage. She whooped, "Praise the Lord," loud enough to catch his attention and waved her hands up in the air. Angie sat sullenly, her arms crossed over her chest. She was wearing her only dress—a red and white polka-dotted number that she wore to go out dancing. The bottom of the hem only just cleared her rear and the spaghetti straps kept slipping off of her shoulders.

"Turn your ra-dio on, get in touch with Je-sus." A man with two teeth in his mouth twanged away on a guitar while everyone sang along.

As the final notes of the song died away, Gertie Haywood mounted the platform at the far end of the hall. He had the head and body of a grasshopper. Big eyeballs bulged out of his bald head, perched on top of a long, skinny neck.

"Turn in your swords," he chuckled, "I mean your Bibles, to Hebrews, the eleventh chapter, the first verse. Thank you Jesus! Now this is the Heroes of Faith chapter. Y'all know what a hero is, I suppose."

"Amen," Granny answered back in response.

"Oh brother," Angie grumbled and rolled her eyes.

I thought back to Greek and Roman mythology, to mortal man and divine gods both so riddled with flaws that it was hard to tell the two apart. Here again, as Gertie pointed out, were saints that acted just like sinners. It was a wonder anything got done in the

Kingdom of God. There was Cain and Abel, the first
fruit of Adam and Eve, duking it out with each other
until finally Cain killed Abel, committing the first
murder on planet Earth. There was old Abraham and
Sarah who both had a hard time believing God would
give them an heir. Not trusting God, Abraham snuck
off with his servant girl and nine months later along
came Ishmael. Jacob stole his brother's birthright and
tricked his blind father. Moses had to lead Israel around
in the desert for forty years because they didn't have
enough faith. On and on, Gertie told one discouraging
story after another about God urging one of his people
to do something and that person turning right around
and doing the opposite. They were more like cowards
of the faith rather than heroes.

"'Now faith,'" Gertie quoted from his open Bible,
"'is the substance of things hoped for, the evidence of
things not seen.'"

"Hallelujah!" exclaimed Granny.

Angie pulled a nail file out of her purse and began
to grind down her cuticles.

Things not seen. There were so many things out
there, beyond the ridge, beyond my reach, beyond
books. Worlds words cannot describe, mixed up with
the stars—dreams and wishes, hopes and plans.

"We are surrounded," Gertie thundered, "by these

witnesses. It says so here in God's word, surrounded by a great, big cloud of witnesses. Ever be in a fog and can't make your way out, can't see your hand in front of your face? That's how it is, folks, we need others to help us on our way, to be a guiding light and show us the proper path."

As Gertie went on preaching, he got more and more worked up. To emphasize some point he was trying to make he would kick his leg out from behind the podium or wave his arms over his head like floppy grasshopper antennae. "And sometimes the ones to helps us, to show us the light are right around us. They're as close as the nose on your face."

I glanced over at Granny. She was nodding off, her head snapping back and forth like a baby with a weak neck. Angie threw her hand over her mouth, snorting in restrained laughter.

"Therefore," Gertie went on, "let us lay aside every weight, amen, and sin that so easily besets us and run—" He kicked his spindly insect-jointed leg out. "Run the race set before you." Gertie looked out over the flock. "Don't be scared. 'Ye are not of those who shrink back and are destroyed, but those who persevere and endure.' Run!"

By now Gertie's arms were moving faster, and in his hurry to get his words out he sprayed a tiny arc of spittle. I could hear the scraping of chairs behind and before me; fold-up chairs were pushed toward the walls. Mamas passed babies off to neighbors.

Granny was wide-awake, rattling her tambourine. "Save me, save me," she yowled with a shrill note of urgency in her voice.

Here it comes, I thought, the Holy Ghost.

Granny had told me about church services she had attended as a girl growing up in the mountains. All-night camp meetings where you caught the Holy Spirit like it was diphtheria, letting it rage through the body until it had run its course. Evidence of the Spirit was a trembling, a loosening of the tongue. You thought you were speaking English, but the whole time you might be talking Armenian or Zulu or an entirely new language, a language of prayer Granny said, of the soul, utterances too deep for words.

I tried to imagine what that must be like—to come under the spell of the Holy Ghost, where everything dammed up inside bursts out in a stream of baby talk that only God can understand. I waited.

Gertie leveled his finger toward my section of the room. He pointed right at me. "Run you sinner."

Granny spun around like a loose electrical wire, her hair frizzed out. Angie hoisted her dress straps up on her shoulders.

I wanted to speak in other tongues. I wanted to fall out beneath the weight of something greater than myself, to be surrounded by a cloud of witnesses.

"Run to Jesus, ye of little faith."

That was me—so low in spirit that I couldn't see beyond the hills, the ravine, or the dump outside my own front door.

The guy with the guitar began to play the same three chords over and over while Gertie continued to holler, "Run to the everlasting arms of Jesus, dear ones!" He swung his arms wide open. He had his flock whipped into a frenzy. People around me started a stampede toward the altar.

It seemed so easy. All I had to do was believe. But that was exactly the problem. I found it impossible to step outside the walls of rationality, to rise above my skepticism. God, I prayed, help my unbelief.

I felt a rustling beside me. Angie stepped around me and made a dash for the altar, tears streaming down her face.

"Glory be!" Granny whirled.

The whole room was charged with Holy Ghost fever. Grown men were down on their knees weeping and women were at the front begging for the Spirit to fall.

I gripped the back of the chair in front of me. Perhaps it was as simple as "letting go and letting God in."

Gertie laid his hand on the heads of those who had gone forward. They toppled like bowling pins beneath his touch. He got to Angie and prayed over her. The words sounded strangely like he was saying rapid-fire, She came on a Honda, she came on a Honda.

Angie's knees buckle as she fell over backwards.

Granny hooted. "She's got it, Lordy, she's done got it."

Angie lay passed out at Gertie Haywood's feet, her polka-dot dress had accidentally ridden up, revealing her under panties—red devils holding pitchforks with the words "the Devil made me do it."

I sank down into my seat, praying for a sinkhole to open and swallow me.

15

Prospects of Great
Expectations

Gertie left town without even considering Granny's proposal of domestic bliss. Maybe he had an inkling it would be more like domestic abuse. Granny got over her disappointment soon enough and went back to making life in the trailer difficult for everyone around her. Daddy's trial hadn't gone well. He was still in jail. Something about not co-operating. He blamed his lawyer, a young girl just out of law school. She must have been smart enough to see that Daddy was slippery. Mama had been up to see him twice. Once Angie drove and another time Mama took the bus to Columbus and then drove back the truck, which was finally released from the police pound.

At the end of English class one afternoon Ms. Knudsen asked a few of us to stay back. Hassan, Patty, and Kyle, plus three others from our gifted class, Riley McGuire, Vijay, and Ginger, we all gathered around Ms. Knudsen as she stood leaning back against her desk. She wore slacks with leather Earth shoes to school every day when most of the other lady teachers were still in the habit of wearing skirts and dresses.

"I have a proposition for you," she began. "Relax. It's not bad. In fact, I think it's great. Have you heard about *Whiz Kidz*?" she asked.

I nodded. Not because I was into it, but because— well, it's like saying interesting. Mostly I wanted to fit in with the others, who were all nodding their heads.

"I'm putting together a team to represent Athens Middle School."

We looked at each other.

"Listen I know it'll be a lot of work. There will be drills and practices every day after school for the next two weeks. It means you'll all have to work together." I glanced past Kyle at Hassan and telepathically communicated "us two."

Ms. Knudsen went on, "If we win Regionals, the two best students get to advance to the State competition held in Columbus. Each State finalist will receive a $5,000 scholarship. For the college of their choice."

Me! Me! my heart screamed, waving its twiggy arteries for attention.

"And, of course, you'll get to go on TV. We'll start with the seven of you and then pare down to five for Regionals." She tossed her thick brown hair back over her shoulders, revealing huge hoop earrings with little crescent moons dangling inside. "What'da ya say, kids?"

"Sure," Patty volunteered first, "sounds great."

"I'm game," said Kyle.

Riley pulled out his daytime planner and flipped over a couple of pages. "I have the next few of weeks free. When can I pencil in the first match?"

"That will be in a week and a half against Stuart Elementary."

"Oh, man. We're going to cream those guys," I gloated.

"I knew I could count on you Roland," Ms. Knudsen said.

I was used to being the last one chosen for kickball. It was great to finally be essential for a team.

If I did well in the *Whiz Kidz* competition and made it all the way to the state playoffs, I'd be eligible for the college scholarship. Runner-ups would be given a play-at-home version of the *Whiz Kidz* trivia game. I couldn't imagine playing *Whiz Kidz* at home.

Just as I crested the hill coming up to our trailer the sun broke through the clouds and a golden glow spread over the hillside. There in front of me was a sea of purple violets run rampant and an ocean of tiny yellow and white blossoms and clover growing wild. I got goosebumps. It was as if the Holy Spirit had come upon me.

Mama came out front on the porch. I waved at her. "Do you see them?" I shouted. "The violets over yonder."

She nodded her head, taking her time to speak. "Yes, and the dogwoods are a-bloomin'. You can see in their petals the scars of the cross, the nail prints in Christ's hands."

Her eyes scanned the horizon. "Roland, I've got some bad news." I waited while she paused.

"Your daddy's sick. He's up in the Columbus Hospital bad off."

The moment of glory had passed; heavy clouds once again obscured the sun.

"It's his lungs, honey."

Mama reached out to touch me, but I backed away.

"The doctors say it ain't good, but what do they really know?"

"This is all my fault."

"Don't be ridiculous, Roland. Your Daddy has smoked most of his life."

"I drove him off." I closed my eyes, shutting out Mama and the gray clouds.

"Look at me son."

I opened my eyes.

"That just ain't true."

Mama gazed off, following the flight of a swallow-tailed kite as it darted and dived from bush to branch to fence post. "He sets great store by you. That's why he acts the way he does."

I didn't say it, but I thought, you mean making me feel not quite as good as the others. As if being with me was painful, a chore to be endured. I could see it in his eyes, the way they went blank as if he were somewhere else in his head, in time.

I lay in bed that night listening to the trailer pop and creak and Mama's heavy footsteps. I thought about Daddy sick up in a Columbus hospital room. He'd traded one prison for another. I had a feeling, something terrible and heavy pressing down on me in bed. Daddy wasn't going to come home. Death, I reckoned, is a lot like crossing fence lines. My melancholy thoughts sent shivers down my body and I pulled my blanket up over my head.

When the county ran the phone lines out to our trailer I was ever fascinated by the idea that right outside my door, through those tiny wires, people from far away could communicate to one another. I used to go outside in the dead of night when everyone else was asleep and lie down beneath the wires and listen to them hum. I imagined a woman in New York City talking to her boyfriend in Parkersburg, West Virginia, or perhaps a man in Columbus talking to his son in California. In the mornings I'd awake stone cold and shivering, my body soaked from the heavy dew. I'd stretch my muscles, unable to rid myself of the awful aching inside of me.

If only I could I would shrink myself down and flow through those wires to Daddy's bedside.

Every day for the next week and a half we all got together with Ms. Knudsen in her classroom after school, where she went over the *Whiz Kidz* handbook. *Whiz Kidz* teams are composed of students who excel in math, literature, music and art, geography, history and government, science, and current events. During the first round, questions are discharged in a rapid-fire format. A player signals if they would like to answer.

If answered incorrectly the opposing team gets a turn to answer. Points are awarded for each correct answer. The second round is a little more complicated, but if worked right a team can earn up to fifty points. The second round begins with a five-point toss up question, which, if answered correctly, allows the team to advance to another level. The questions get increasingly more difficult.

As Ms. Knudsen fired practice questions, there was a sense of friendly rivalry among us as we scrambled to be the first to answer. Kyle liked to pound his fist on his desk to get Ms. Knudsen's attention. Patty would sit with her back straight and shoot her hand up into the air like the Statue of Liberty. Ginger, who was normally mousy and shy, was a fierce competitor, shouting out answers over Hassan, who at first was too polite. Eventually, though, he became just as cutthroat as the rest of us. Riley's mind worked like a calculator, seizing numbers and dates—you could see it in his eyes, spinning around like a slot machine lining up cherries and oranges—computing the problems, and spitting back answers.

Ms. Knudsen brought a treat for us, something made with whole-wheat flour and honey because she thought white flour and refined sugar were basically poison.

The district competition was to take place on the campus of Ohio University. We got out of school early in order to get there an hour before the competition started. It felt odd walking through town when our middle school classmates were still stuck inside of school. The sidewalks were crowded with college students in cut-offs and T-shirts sporting spring-break tans. I'd heard from Kyle and Hassan that in college, a student has the choice of what classes to take, where they will sit, and can even arrange their schedule around late mornings and long weekends. More than ever I wanted to go to college and be one of those lucky students.

The third floor of McCracken Hall was buzzing with *Whiz Kidz*. I recognized former classmates from Stuart. I considered going over and saying hey, but thought better of it. It wouldn't look cool fraternizing with the enemy even if we were going to beat the tar out of them.

"Now, listen up, guys," Ms. Knudsen rallied us. I was glad to be representing Athens Middle School. Ms. Knudsen was the prettiest teacher there, and our team was the best dressed. Hassan and Vijay both wore Chino pants and Izod shirts. Ginger wore a dress suit and Riley McGuire with his thin hair wetted and combed back looked like a state senator. Even Patty was all-business in a blouse paired with black slacks. I folded my arms over my chest in an attempt to cover up my T-shirt, a Pony's Pizza delivery shirt that Larry had left behind.

A moderator called the room to order and quickly reviewed the rules. "Absolutely no consultation will be allowed during the first and fourth rounds. After a player buzzes in, he or she must first be recognized before answering. There will be a five-point penalty assessed on any player who buzzes in and attempts to answer before the question is completely read. If the reader is in the middle of the last word, it is up to the judges to assess the penalty."

It seemed to me that there were rules governing the rules. While the moderator droned on and on, I sized up our opponents across from us. Their little ferret faces were rigid, their eyes fraught with fear.

"If a player gets unruly, the proctor may issue a warning. Cussing, beating your head against the table, and inappropriate gestures are grounds for ejection." The speaker looked over his bifocals, which had slipped down to the tip of his nose. "Any questions?"

Hassan whispered to me, "And no puking."

I muffled laughter.

The first round began.

"The area of a circle 6 meters in diameter exceeds the combined areas of a circle 4 meters in diameter and a circle 2 meters in diameter by how many square meters?"

Riley buzzed in first. "4 pi." He blinked as if resetting his calculator-brain.

"The United States government is comprised of how many branches?"

We all pounced on the buzzer, yet Ginger shouted over all of us. "Three!"

Athens Middle School answered every toss-up question, never even giving Stuart a chance to ring in. We entered the second round with a total of 10 points and managed to rack up fifty more. For the sixty-second scare-your-pants-off third round, I buzzed in so much I felt like I was getting a blister on my finger. I helped our team earn a whopping twenty points plus a twenty-point bonus for answering all ten questions. Stuart Elementary missed every other question, often mumbling, *Pass*, or *I don't know*. They managed to score only twenty-five points.

WONNGG! The final bell rang, and Athens had won a resounding victory.

The kids on the Stuart team heaved a long sigh. Some laid their heads down on top of the table. I wondered if things might have ended differently had I been on their team. Which was better, I tried to puzzle out—to be the smartest student at Stuart or one of many gifted students at Athens Middle School? I knew the right answer to that question when Ms. Knudsen invited us all uptown for milkshakes—on her!

The sunshine felt good on my neck and arms as I sat outside on a low wall next to Patty and Hassan, sipping my shake. I tucked the short sleeves of my T-shirt under like a farmer. Patty's hair blazed platinum in the bright light.

"What flavor do you have?" she asked. When she opened her mouth to speak her white teeth almost blinded me. For a split second I couldn't remember what I'd ordered.

"Strawberry."

"Really? I love strawberry. Can I have a taste?" Without waiting for an answer she leaned over and delicately placed her lips on my straw.

"Mmm, that *is* good." She wiped her lips with the back of her hand and smiled. "Would you like a sip of mine? It's peanut butter and triple chocolate fudge coffee."

I stared at the impression left behind by her shiny lip gloss.

"I'll try it," Hassan piped up. He reached for her tall styrofoam cup and sucked up a mouthful. "Wow! Want to try some, Roland?"

My eyes were glued to my straw and the trace of her lips.

"Roland, you did a great job today. Think you can do even better against Logan next week at Regionals?" Patty asked.

"Yeah," I answered her out of a sublime and self-satisfied subconscious.

No Ruz

Spring hit Mama's garden full force—everything was blooming: black-eyed Susans, panda-eyed pansies, and daisies with bee-hive centers. I moved Granny's old chair out onto the cement-slab porch.

It was spring break and I had called Hassan to see if he wanted to get together for a study session. Lord knows I couldn't invite him to the trailer, so we arranged to meet in the pine grove.

Through the brush I heard the clatter of a large animal thrashing about. I started up—what in the world? —when Hassan stumbled into the clearing.

"I said I'd remember how to get back here," he boasted, then added, "Happy New Year."

"Huh?"

"According to the Muslim calendar this is the time for the new year, *No Ruz*, spring when all things are made new again. It makes sense, doesn't it?"

"Yeah, I guess." I knew better than to say *interesting*.

Hassan took a colorful scarf out of his backpack and spread it on the ground. "We have a tradition," he began. On top of the scarf he placed a hard-boiled egg. "Where we eat specific foods. The egg represents new life just as these do—" He plucked a couple of burs and catbriers off of his soccer shirt and placed them on the scarf. "Seeds."

Next from his bag he brought out a baggie of goldfish crackers. "Usually we use real goldfish, but these will have to do, and this is called a *noghl*," he said holding up a small chewy raisin cake, which reminded me of a Fig Newton cookie. "These objects all begin with the same letter of the alphabet in Farsi."

I sat back on my haunches. "This coming Sunday will be Easter," I said, trying not to think about Daddy, wishing he could come home.

Hassan continued. "About a week or so before the New Year my mother and sisters clean the whole house, from top to bottom. They beat the dirt out of the rugs, sweep the dust out of all the corners, and wash down the windows and walls. Everything must be fresh and new. My mother makes a special uncooked wheat cake."

"Does it taste good?"

"You don't eat it. That would be awful. In it are whole grains of wheat. The cake is in layers, one for each member of the family. The unbaked cake is kept moist so that the wheat sprouts and begins to grow. Soon the cake becomes a beautiful green thing."

"Sort of like a Chia pet?" I asked.

Hassan stared at me. "It's just a symbol."

"Gotcha."

"On the thirteenth day of the New Year the family takes this wheat cake outside and throws it away, and with it goes all the bad feelings and quarreling in the home."

I needed a cake for every time Angie pulled up in her Trans Am. If only it were that easy to rid the trailer of Granny's foul moods.

"Anything else?" I asked.

Hassan plucked a blade of grass. "Then the family weaves a chain of grass. For each blade of grass a good wish is made."

I wished a wish, a chain of them, enough to bring Daddy home from the hospital.

Hassan also produced from his backpack apples and dried fruits and a baggie of nuts.

"Pistachios and almonds. A feast for us," he said,

waving his hand over the scarf.

Together we celebrated the new year by eating the items before us.

Back at school we only had a week until the upcoming Regionals. We prepped at school as a team. In addition, Hassan asked if I'd like to come over to his house for some intensive drilling.

I rode down Congress Avenue on my clunker bike to the part of town where professors mostly lived. His house was a two-story red brick with ivy growing up the walls. I rang the bell and a woman who looked like Hassan with the same dark eyes answered the door.

"Come in Roland," she greeted me. "I will call down Hassan."

She had an accent and pronounced Hassan's name differently, not as flat as we were used to saying it at school. "Have a seat," she offered.

In front of the couch on a low coffee table was a dish filled with bright red pistachios. On a stand next to a Lazy-Boy recliner was a stack of weekly news magazines. On the cover of one of them was a picture of the Ayatollah Khomeini glaring beneath his furry eyebrows. At one end of the room bookshelves were built into the wall. I had never seen so many hardcover books, spines dark blue, forest green, a stately red.

Hassan bounded into the room. Mrs. Reza left to fetch refreshments and returned with two glasses of lemonade and some sugar cookies on a tray. In the middle of our snack Hassan's sisters came home from high school. Like most girls they talked a lot, switching back and forth from English to Farsi. Hassan's mother turned to me. "More lemonade, Roland?"

Hassan checked his wristwatch. "Mother, we have to study."

"Okay, all right. You can go."

On the way up the stairs I whispered to Hassan, "Why aren't your mom and sisters wearing one of those things?"

"A *chador*? There is no need to in the home. When she goes out in public she wears a covering and then only a headscarf. Before we left Iran this was typical. Women dressed modern, but modest. Now we hear that the hardliners insist that women be completely covered."

Hassan opened the door to his room. He had his own bed, his own dresser, and his own bookshelf. On top of Hassan's desk was what looked like a box with the words KAYPRO on the side.

"What's that?" I asked.

"A computer," Hassan answered, unfastening the sides. The lid came off to become a keyboard while the oblong box was like a TV with a screen. He flipped a power switch in the back and up popped a worm's nest of green lettering. The machine chugged along as if it were actually thinking. "I wish I could play games on it. The grad students up at the Accelerator Lab where my father works play Space Invaders on the mainframe. It's so cool!"

I had no idea what Hassan was talking about. After a second the screen cleared and he typed in a code. "You see, I can type here and it goes there, and the information is stored inside or else on a floppy disc, and then when I'm ready I can ask for it to print and it comes out here." He turned on the printer. I took a step back when it began to slingshot back and forth across a scroll of perforated paper coming up from a box underneath his desk.

"Sure looks handier than an electric typewriter."

We sat down on the floor and leaned against his bed. I held the *Whiz Kidz* handbook in front of me and fed a round of made-up questions at Hassan. "What country eats all the time?"

"Buzz. Hungary."

"What is a mathematician's favorite dessert?"

"Buzz. Pi."

"Who's buried in Grant's tomb?"

"Abraham Lincoln?"

BUZZZZZ.

"You're pretty good," I said. His English had improved, in the sense that he got stupid jokes now.

Hassan beamed. "Thanks. The hardest category for me is literature. I'm not so familiar with your stories. Perhaps, you could tutor me."

I tried to think. There are so many stories, but one author our class hadn't studied yet was Dickens. "There's this book I read last summer, *Great Expectations.*"

"Tell it," asked Hassan.

I stared up at the ceiling. "Well, it's the story of a poor boy named Pip—"

"Pip?"

"Yeah."

Hassan wrote the name down in a notebook. "A strange name."

"It's a nickname. He always wanted to go places, become a gentleman. But in the process of improving himself, he drifted away from the people who cared the most about him, Joe and Biddy."

"Biddy?"

"Yeah, and Estella, the girl he was infatuated with, but who didn't give a twit for him. She played him like he was a deck of cards, called him names, and made fun of him because he was from the sticks—"

"The sticks?"

"The boonies—"

"What?"

"*Anyway*, she made him feel inferior. One day Pip came into a lot of money, his expectations, but instead of becoming a better person, he squandered his fortune on stuff." I looked around the room. I wished I had a computer and a library of gleaming, brand-new books. "All along he thought it was Miss Havisham, a rich neighbor lady, helping him out, but it wasn't—it was someone else."

"Who?"

Here's where it got weirder and harder to explain. "A prisoner named Magwitch."

I was right. Hassan had stopped writing things down. "Anyway, Pip loses everything. He tries to go back to his family and village, but he doesn't fit in. No longer able to live as a gentleman, yet he can't exactly go back to being a blacksmith's apprentice. All that is left for him is to leave town and live on his own."

Hassan sighed. "Your English stories are always so full of defeat. They like to show the side of people that isn't the most favorable. I'd much rather read about brave kings and great deeds and bloody battles."

I agreed.

"In Iran we were taught to read the *Shahnameh*."

"What's that?" I asked.

"A long poem that contains stories about our

ancient Persian history. Sort of like mythology. All about our kings and their glorious accomplishments."

"And you memorized this poem?"

"Of course not. It's much too long—maybe ten times the size of *The Diary of Anne Frank* or *The Odyssey*. No, we had to memorize lines from the poem." He closed his eyes and began to recite in Farsi. After a second he opened his eyes. "I guess that doesn't mean much to you. Let me see if I can translate.

> *When dawn burst forth from out the eastern sky,*
> *Ripping apart the darkness of the night,*
> *Prince Minuchihr came forth out from the ranks,*
> *Wearing his chest armor, sword, and helmet.*

The words came faltering at first. Soon, though, stanzas poured out of him, smooth and strong. He spoke as if the images were stored in his mind, on a floppy disc.

Both armies advanced like mountains from their base,

> *A battle cry rang out on either side;*
> *The plain became a bloody sea,*
> *You might say that blood-red tulips sprang*
> *from the earth.*

In streams of gore the elephants stood, knee-deep,
Mounted as if on red pedestals.
The air was clogged with fog from the horsemen's dust,
Their gleaming swords of steel flashed like lightning,
As if the sky was on fire,
The earth's surface shone diamond-like with flame.

I lay listening, picturing men on sweat-flanked horses charging over the sand with their long scarves flying. "Cool. It sort of reminds me of *Star Wars*." The second installment of the trilogy was due on screen any day.

Hassan's eyes lit up. "Ever since the first movie, I've been dying to find out what's next for Han Solo and the Rebel Forces."

And, of course, Luke seemed to have things pretty well in hand for winning Princess Leia. "Just like your poem, *Star Wars* is a whole world, a place not like here."

Hassan thought for a second. "Even though it doesn't exist, I can imagine myself there."

Did he mean ancient Persia or a galaxy far away? *Great Expectations* is the same, I guess. Boy leaves home, boy hopes to make good, boy returns. The only thing that changes is this: Will he be a hero or a failure?

The smell of spicy hamburger cooking wafted up to Hassan's room telling us it was almost suppertime.

We went downstairs where Hassan's father sat in the Lazy-Boy watching TV. He got up to greet me.

After shaking my hand, Mr. Reza said, "There's been an accident." We turned toward the TV set.

Images played across the console behind him—a TV of which all the knobs were in place. News clips showed a burning helicopter and scattered smoking wreckage. Mr. Reza removed his glasses, and his eyes immediately became smaller.

"Eight servicemen have been killed. It was a military mission meant to rescue the Americans held hostage in the embassy, but things went terribly wrong."

Mr. Reza's eyes blurred. "The helicopters ran into a sand storm and as they withdrew there was a collision."

I didn't understand. America was supposed to be a "superpower." We had technology and million-dollar weaponry; we had bombs and missiles, radar and geographic homing devices. Where was the victory, the lightning flash of gleaming steel swords? We were the good guys. But this wasn't *Star Wars* or the *Shahnameh*; it was real life, on TV, breaking news. I couldn't help feeling downhearted.

Mrs. Reza invited me to stay to dinner.

"Thank you, ma'am, but I've got to get home." It had been such a long time since I'd had actual meat.

Mama had been stretching our food stamps by making biscuits and SPAM gravy a couple times a week.

"Perhaps another time," she said.

The Empire Strikes Back

The Empire Strikes Back was exactly what I needed to take my mind off Daddy. He had called a couple of times using a telephone in his hospital room. I could tell by the way he struggled in between words that he was fighting for air.

By seven o'clock p.m. practically every kid from Athens Middle School and Stuart Elementary was at the Athenaeum movie theater for the opening of the film. The line stretched halfway down the street, all the way back to the Bagel Buggy parked in front of the Ohio University campus gateway. Mama had somehow scrounged up a few stray dollars for me, even though Hassan had offered to pay my way. I was a bit like

Daddy in that I'd rather cut off my hand than take a hand-out. Even though he was a rascal, Daddy wasn't a freeloader.

Once in the theater Hassan and I rushed for the balcony. Before the movie started Hassan spied Kyle a few rows below and pelted him with Jujubes. Just as he turned around to see where the hard little jelly candies were coming from, the lights went down and the big screen lit up.

It had been three years since the destruction of the Death Star, and Luke was now commander of the Rebel Alliance. Within minutes of the film's opening a huge ice creature that sort of resembled an abominable snowman captured Luke and carried him to a snow cave to torture him. Luke sure did take a beating.

The plot took more twists and turns than Larry in an automobile. Just like in our unit on myths, where the gods had devised a way to defeat mortals and leave them humbled, circumstances worked against and sometimes for Luke and Han. Hassan and I left the theater in a daze.

"Can you believe that?" asked Hassan, referring to Luke Skywalker's father.

I shook my head. I'd always had one idea of who my daddy was, and now slowly this picture was changing. It's complicated.

Hassan ran ahead of me, vanquishing lampposts and garbage cans with an imaginary lightsaber. "Schroom, schroom." He mimicked the sound effect from the movie. He took aim at my head, pretending to lop it off.

"Cut it out." I wasn't in the mood.

Hassan looked hurt. "Hey, I'm just playing."

"Exactly."

"What's bothering you?" Hassan was walking backwards down the sidewalk, facing me. I was thinking about Daddy and the Dark Side.

"Han Solo is cooler than Luke," Hassan stated.

I shrugged. "Now he is, I guess," I said, reflecting on the last scenes where he was frozen.

Hassan laughed, getting my meaning. "Not *that* way."

All over town were little yellow ribbons, wrapped around lamp posts, stop signs, and mailboxes. People had tied them there in hopes that the hostages would soon be released.

"My parents got word today. My uncle is in jail and my aunt has had to go into hiding."

"Whoa," I said. "That's rough." I debated telling Hassan about Daddy when suddenly Kyle showed up over Hassan's shoulder. He put his finger up to his mouth so I wouldn't tip Hassan off.

"Uh—" I stopped walking.

Kyle crept up behind Hassan with his hood up around his face like Darth Vader and grabbed the back of Hassan's pants and performed the galactic of all middle school super moves. A wedgie.

Hassan's eyes bulged in surprise. He fought with his pants, trying to get them out of his crack.

I couldn't help laughing. Kyle, too, doubled over.

The only one who didn't think it was funny was Hassan. His face reddened. "You traitor," he said, looking right at me.

I flinched as if he had slapped me.

Hassan ran to grab his bike parked to the side of the movie house.

Kyle turned to me. "I guess the dude's never had a wedgie before." He continued laughing, a high-pitched titter.

"Shut up Kyle." I was mad at him. And at myself.

I picked up my clunker and took off after Hassan. I rode up Congress Avenue, breathing hard, trying to catch him. On a steep downhill I picked up so much speed the bike shimmied and shook beneath me, making me feel that at any minute I might lose control and careen off into someone's yard.

I found him sitting on the steps leading to his porch. "Hey," I said, dropping my bike into the grass.

"Why didn't you warn me?"

"I'm sorry. It was stupid. I'm stupid." I paused. "I didn't know he was going to do that."

"The kids at school think I'm a terrorist. You should see how they look at me, out of the corner of their eyes, like they don't trust me. I see how they walk around me in the hallways as if I might shoot them or something."

He scuffed his tennis shoes along the cement pavement. "I hate Kyle. I hate this place."

I sat down on the first step, below him. I tried to think of something to say. "Luke Skywalker was kind of a disappointment."

Hassan pushed his bangs out of his eyes. "If only I could get people to like me."

"Me and Patty—"

"You're the only ones. Now, I don't know."

"People think that because I live in a trailer I'm ignorant, a hillbilly."

"At least you aren't a foreigner."

"They call me trailer trash. The way they say it makes it sound like bad body odor."

"Well, at least you can go home."

I didn't want to admit it. "That's not such a big deal."

Hassan looked up. "I'm stuck here."

"We both are." I tried to think. "You've got to make them see you for who you really are."

"Oh, yeah, like what? The enemy of the free world?"

"Just win the *Whiz Kidz* contest. Listen, we'll go to the Regionals next Wednesday where you'll blow the other team away."

Hassan didn't look too convinced.

"Look, Hassan," I said, moving my arm like I was slicing the air with a lightsaber. "The Force will be with us."

I Am Not Pip

Mama came out into the kitchen wearing her Ziggy nightgown. The pajama material was worn thin and stretched over her broad bottom and protruding tummy. "You're up late. Burning the midnight oil as we used to say."

I squinted up at her through the glare of a kerosene lamp. A few days ago the county had switched off the electricity to the trailer. I looked up from the *Whiz Kidz* handbook I'd been studying at the kitchen table and rubbed my eyes. "I want to do good at the contest tomorrow."

Mama reached out and pushed my hair back. She scruffed the front of it like she used to when I was younger. "This is important to you, is it?"

I nodded. "If I make it all the way to the state finals, I'll have a chance for a college scholarship."

"Son, I'll be praying for you. It's where you belong, away from here." Then she added, "Your daddy will be pleased."

I closed the creased and battered manual. Phone calls were getting harder and harder for Daddy. I had told him all about being a Whiz Kid and beating Stuart Elementary and walking uptown for milk shakes. He didn't seem impressed. "You are. So much. Smarter than some. Contest," he said in a halting, raspy voice. I sure hoped he was going to get better, but I was starting to wonder.

I turned down the lantern and stood up to go to bed. For a second the wick continued to glow before finally extinguishing itself.

A little yellow school bus about half the size of a regular one pulled up in front of Athens Middle School to transport us whizzies to Logan Middle School. I climbed on board and took a seat in the back.

As we rode along I stared out the window. My mind was in a whirl and my stomach was a mess. I'd heard the phrase "butterflies in the stomach" before, but this felt more like alligators wrestling.

The road to Logan was narrow in places, only two lanes with no shoulder. A canopy of trees shaded the black asphalt, creating a tunnel effect, then, all at once, the bus would burst out into bright sunlight where spring-green soybean fields bordered both sides of the road. Planted in the middle of these fields were pumpjacks. The same land that produced high sulfur coal also produced a low-grade oil, trapped beneath layers of shale, sand, and stone. The pumps zigzagging up and down reminded me of an ornament Larry had on the rear dash of his car—a plastic bird dressed in a tuxedo and top hat, which bobbed his beak back and forth into a fake martini glass.

Hassan moved back to sit in front of me. "Nervous?" he asked.

Pow! Pow! An alligator snapped its jaws and swished its tail, searing the lining of my stomach.

Before boarding the bus, Ms. Knudsen had explained that only five students would be allowed to compete this afternoon. She was planning to make substitutions to try and give everyone a chance. Depending on if Athens won, she would have to figure out which of us to send on to Columbus for the state semifinals and finals. I desperately wanted to make the cut, be part of that elite team.

Out beyond the oil pumps was an old barn leaning

to one side, ready to collapse. The weather and sun had bleached the wood the color of old bones. The high barn roof had caved in to where I could see clear through the skeletal ribs of the trussed rafters.

No one would expect a hillbilly to make it to the state finals. I'd like to surprise them all, show them what I'm made of. I imagined walking in the door and receiving a hero's welcome. Mama would cook my favorite, fried chicken and mashed potatoes, and Granny might take a night off from being grumpy. Once Angie heard that I was going to State she'd have to pay me a little more respect and quit telling me all the time that she was going to kick my butt. News of my victory would perk Daddy up so much the doctors would have to release him, send him home with me from Columbus.

"Hey!" Patty plopped down next to me.

I sat bolt upright.

"What's going on?" she queried.

"Nothing."

"I just wanted to say good luck."

"Thanks," I said. I thought of Pip with his great expectations. This was probably how he felt, on the brink of some bright future. If only.

After a minute of awkward silence, Patty turned around in her seat next to Hassan.

Damn, damn, damn. I was such a jerk.

171

The gymnasium at Logan was a lot smaller and more rustic than I expected. There weren't even any bleachers for the parents and school officials to sit on. Chairs were arranged around the perimeter of the basketball court. In the center, on top of a tarp to protect the parquet floor, several tables faced each other. A podium was dragged out between the two tables and a hush fell over the room as the announcer approached the microphone.

"Is this thing on?" A spindly man with big horse teeth yelled into the microphone. "Check, check."

I heard him loud and clear and so did the alligators doing back flips. Hassan waved to his parents; they waved back. I was glad my family wasn't there. I could just see Granny cursing and waving her four-legged cane.

Ms. Knudsen sent Vijay, Riley, Ginger, Hassan, and Patty in first, while Kyle and I sat out round one.

The man at the microphone finished going over the rules of play and introduced the moderator, a prissy schoolmarm-looking lady with cat eyeglasses and a sweater draped over her shoulders. She began by firing off questions in a no-monkey-business voice.

"The Battle of Waterloo was fought in what year?"

Patty's hand shot up, while Ginger hit the buzzer. "1815."

A point for Athens Middle School.

"And who won the Battle of Waterloo?"

Logan rang in first. "Napoleon surrendered to the Duke of Wellington."

"I'll accept that. England."

It went on like this, back and forth. I hated sitting it out. My finger itched to press an imaginary bell. At the end of round one the score was tied.

"Round Two," the moderator announced. "Athens, please pick a category. Remember, consultation is allowed, but you must remain seated."

Ms. Knudsen sent in Kyle for Riley who hadn't answered a single question. Kyle sat next to Patty. I watched them lean in together. "Geography."

"For five points, name the capital of Indonesia?"

"Jakarta," Hassan buzzed in.

"What is the number one export of Indonesia?"

They whispered amongst themselves. "Rubber?" guessed Patty. "Coconuts?" Kyle said. "No, no." Hassan shook his head. He hit the buzzer. "Oil."

"Correct. Identify the mountain range found along eastern New Guinea."

Really? These questions were crazy hard. Who would know the answer—

Once again Hassan got to the buzzer first. "The Jayawijaya Mountains."

"In 1883 this infamous volcano erupted off the Sunda Strait?"

"Krakatoa!" Kyle looked around like he was hot stuff, but no one was paying any attention. We needed one more answer in order to clinch the round.

"And finally, for twenty-five points. Indonesia was formerly a colony of what nation?"

"Great Britain," Logan answered. No.

Hassan wasted no time consulting. "The Netherlands."

Wow! Athens had racked up 75 points. Patty cheered and high-fived Hassan.

Next it was Logan's turn. They had a student who reminded me of Hassan's Kaypro, spouting answers in a robotic fashion. Even his voice was a flat monotone. Basically he was the whole team, answering all the questions right. I wanted to find the OFF switch.

Ms. Knudsen subbed me in for Ginger for the rapid-fire third round. We were still tied with Logan.

The reader straightened her sweater, which had started to drift off her narrow shoulders. "Who was the first man to orbit the earth?"

Hassan got to the bell first. "John Glenn."

"No, sorry."

Hassan looked baffled.

The Logan team rebounded. "Yuri Gagarin."

"Correct." She looked directly at Hassan. "Not the first American in orbit. Name the monk who experimented with hereditary traits using garden peas."

Patty rang in and shouted, "Gregor Mendel!" Then added under her breath, "Easy-peasy."

"Correct. Next question: This country was originally called the Congo—"

"Zaire," Hassan answered confidently.

"Please wait for the question to be completely read." She began again, "This country, which was originally known as the Congo, became Zaire in what year? Logan you have the option." Logan again answered correctly.

The score was Athens 83 and Logan 85. Hassan wiped a build-up of moisture from his upper lip.

"Which American president coined the term 'New Deal'?"

Hassan rang the bell and hesitated. "Roosevelt."

"I'm sorry that answer is incorrect."

Oh, man, I silently pushed. *Cm'on!*

The other team rang in. "*Franklin Delano* Roosevelt?"

"That is correct. You are aware that two different Roosevelts served as president and that you must identify the right one."

Hassan had already cost us three points. He rolled up the sleeves on his shirt in preparation for the next question. I looked over at the sidelines. Mr. Reza paced the floor while Hassan's mother sat in a chair wringing the ends of her headscarf.

"Name the rock band nicknamed the 'mop tops'."

I slammed on the poor bell. "The Beatles." The alligators inside of me finally took a break.

"This artist took to painting a series of sunflowers shortly after cutting off his e—"

"Vincent Van Gogh," I shouted.

"I'll allow that since I had nearly completed the last word. Next question—"

WONNGG! *Whew!* I'd managed to tie the game before the bell. Again we were in a dead heat.

Hassan scrubbed his face with his hands as if trying to wake up. I held my breath, waiting to see if she would take out Hassan before round four started.

Round four began with no substitutions. Logan started strong, the giant brain answering three straight in a row, but then something happened and he ran out of batteries. Athens swooped in. Kyle answered, then me. Hassan recovered to contribute. Patty snuck in a final answer before the bell. We held our breath—would it be accepted.

"Correct," the prissy-pants moderator proclaimed.

Patty jumped up. "Oh, my gosh, oh my gosh, ohmygosh! We did it!"

We were rushed by spectators along with Riley,

Ginger, and Vijay from the bench. I melted toward the sidelines. I'd done okay. Yet it was anyone's guess as to who would be selected to go on to Columbus to compete in the semis and finals.

I was tired and hungry walking the last quarter of a mile home after being let out on the gravel road. The sun had set and now all that remained was a lingering twilight. A blue and lavender haze hung over the ridge. As I topped the last hill I saw light coming from the trailer windows.

I walked in and sloughed off my book bag onto the couch. "What's going on?"

Angie sat at the kitchen table painting her nails a bright neon orange. "I paid the light bill," she said, blowing on her fingertips.

Mama was busy cooking at the stove, frying up hamburger that Angie must have brought out from town. "I'm making a special dinner for Angie. Cm'on in Roland and set a spell."

"Oh, no," Granny said mockingly from her chair in the corner of the living room, "he's too busy these days, running around to Fizz Kidz contests. You'd think he was something, the way he's been acting lately. Too big for his britches, he is."

Mama turned on the exhaust fan to let out some

of the grease and smoke. "How'd things go today with your contest and all?"

Before I could answer, Mama interrupted, "Guess what? Angie says she's gonna drive me up to Columbus to see Daddy this weekend."

Angie rolled her eyes. "I said *maybe*. Geez, you'd think Roland could do something around here to help out."

I turned and walked out of the trailer. The stars and black sky seemed to close over me. I was not Pip with the hope of great expectations, just an eighth grader looking for a lucky break.

19

Like an Ancient
Persian Carpet

That night I dreamed the world was coming to an end, and, as most dreams are, mine was confusing. I was at school along with Patty, Hassan, and Kyle Messerhoff. I remember I was talking to Patty, saying something like, So what's the deal with your toe? When suddenly an alarm sounded and Ms. Knudsen rushed into the room where we were to tell us to take cover. I ran like hell across the kickball field where, of course, there was nowhere to hide. Behind me I heard a crack like thunder and a huge explosion, then blinding white light. I did the only thing I could—I dropped down into a drainage ditch between the open field and roadway, and waited. I peeked up over the edge of the trench. Rolling like a dust storm was a nuclear fireball, vaporizing everything in its path, man and beast, trees and buildings. Nothing was spared. I opened my mouth to scream—

Only to be awakened by my radio-alarm clock. I snapped-to in bed, cork-screwed tight in my sweat-soaked sheets, my mouth frozen into a silent ahh, the morning sun blasting and the radio blaring something about an explosion. News that Mount St. Helens out in Washington state had erupted must have worked itself into my dreams. I dragged myself out of bed and pulled on my pants.

Upon arriving at school, Hassan rushed up to me. "I've been here waiting for your bus to arrive."

"What's up?" I kept walking.

"I couldn't sleep last night."

"You and me both." We entered the building together.

"I think I was—how do you say—hyped up from the contest, very excited. As I was trying to go to sleep, I thought and thought."

"I do the same thing," I admitted. "Going back over my day like it was some black and white re-run."

Hassan stopped. "Re-run.?"

"It's a—never mind. Did the volcano get into your dreams too?"

He shook his head. "Do you think we made the team for State?"

Patty closed her locker down the school hallway. Beside her was Kyle.

"I don't know," I answered. Patty and Kyle strolled up to us. I'd been thinking of all the stuff I should have said to her on the bus. Maybe my family was right, maybe I had been thinking only of myself. I called after her. "Hey! Patty. Good luck!"

She turned. "Same to you Roland." She held up two fingers, one wrapped around the other. "Fingers crossed for all of us."

Kyle stood behind her with his fingers in the shape of an L, mouthing the word "loser" to me.

During study hall I made up a flyer. The librarian allowed me to use the copy machine. After school I pasted them up all over town.

EXPERT LAWN CARE. HIRE ME TO CUT YOUR GRASS. REASONABLE RATES. And included our phone number.

Summer was coming. I wouldn't spend it but save it up. The whole way home I calculated how many $5 lawn jobs I'd need in order to get me a mini-bike. I couldn't wait to tell Mama—and to make sure she answered the phone instead of Granny in case customers called.

I was still figuring when I walked into the trailer to find Mama on the couch with a hankie wadded up in her hands. Her eyes were swollen and wet with tears.

"The hospital called."

I waited.

"It's cancer."

After a long pause, I asked, "Is he going to die?"

"They say it's in every part of him."

I forgot about mini-bikes, *Whiz Kidz*, and state finals. My bad dream had come true—it felt like the end of the world.

Ms. Knudsen called me into her classroom after school the next day. "Roland." The way she said my name reminded me of Mama. "Listen I don't know what's going on exactly, but I've heard," she paused, picking and choosing her words, "That things at home aren't easy."

Was she referring to Daddy being in jail, or the lights getting turned off, or the cancer? "Yes ma'am."

She shuddered. "*Really?* I'm a ma'am?"

"Sorry, Ms. Knudsen."

"I just wanted to say how great you've been."

So that's it, I thought, I'm eliminated.

"Congratulations."

There was a ringing in my ears, a fuzzy white noise. I couldn't make sense of her words. "I'm going?"

"Yes. You and Hassan."

When imagining this moment, beating out Kyle, I'd always thought it would feel better. The sweet smell of success. But, ever since getting the news about Daddy, I felt numb. Like, what's the use?

Ms. Knudsen peered at me. "Have you been writing in that notebook I gave you?"

I didn't want to disappoint her. "Sort of."

"Well, if you want to ever share what you've written. I'd love to read it."

I nodded. "Sure." But I meant maybe.

I sat in the back seat next to Hassan staring out the car window. His family had offered to give me a ride. I was glad to not ask Angie for a lift only to hear her whine that she was doing *everything*.

Fields planted in corn swept by, row after row of verdant green stalks separated by the occasional windbreak, poplars or hedge apple trees. I wondered if I should even be there. For some reason I felt like I didn't belong, that it was all a big mistake. Maybe I was being selfish. Maybe I should skip the whole thing.

Hassan broke into my thoughts. "This reminds me of a Persian carpet."

"What?"

"This," he said, pointing out the window, "the landscape."

I had never seen a Persian rug, but I knew about quilts. I guess the patches of green broken up by borders of color could be similar to the patterns on a rug or quilt. Up and down we rode, the black highway a thread, stitched together with railroad tracks and hemmed in by dusty section roads. The telephone wires a daisy chain, looped from pole to pole. A patchwork quilt much like the one Mama had taken up to Columbus to keep Daddy warm in his hospital room.

After a while farms gave way to mini-malls and industrial parks. I recalled the alligators that accompanied me to Regionals. I turned to Hassan. "Are you nervous?"

"It would be a lie to say no," Hassan confessed. "For some reason Regionals seemed way harder."

I nodded. Winning *Whiz Kidz* had faded to the background; all I could think of was how I might work in a visit with Daddy.

Hassan went on, "I'm just glad that's over with."

"Yeah," I agreed.

"Things seem better now. Just the other day Kyle invited me over to his house for an end-of-school party."

I didn't recall getting an invitation—not that I would go.

Hassan's dad pulled into a McDonald's off of High Street for lunch. I had brought some money, but Mr. Reza insisted on paying for my hamburger. After lunch we drove over to Ohio State University where the competition was to take place.

Ohio State University is a much bigger college than Ohio University. We walked around the sprawling campus looking for the journalism building where there was a telecommunications lab with its own studio and radio station. Outside on the green students were playing hacky-sack, lounging under trees, and throwing Frisbees to dogs wearing colorful bandanas around their scruffy necks. We eventually located the right building and took the elevator to the fourth floor.

The elevator doors opened to reveal a mystified Patty. She had on a beige knit T-shirt tucked into a wrap-around skirt and was holding a piece of paper with directions. "Hey!" she said with relief. "This must be the place."

"What are you doing here?" Hassan and I both asked.

"I wanted to wish you luck. Spur you on." She

explained that her aunt lived close to the university. Her mother would hang out there until Patty called for a pick up.

Her smile alone cheered me up. I don't know who felt better by her presence: Hassan or me. Hassan introduced Patty to his parents and as a group we walked down the hallway in search of the TV studio.

Come to find out *Whiz Kidz* was recorded in a closet, actually a room about the size of Mama's bedroom. On my TV screen at home it had seemed way bigger. Hassan and I were part of a much larger team representing southeastern Ohio. We were scheduled to face off against a team comprised of top students from the northeastern conference, from places like Cleveland and Akron. If they were as sharp as they dressed, then we were done for. Each of the members wore pink polo shirts and tan slacks.

Hassan's parents retreated into an adjoining waiting area where they would be able to watch through a huge window. Patty held back a second. None of us said a word until a guy with a radio announcer voice called the room to order.

"Well. Wish me luck," Hassan said with a shaky voice.

"You'll do fine," she said. Patty gave Hassan a hug.

I could see the outline of her bra straps through the fabric. Instead of the alligators, I felt like I was upside down on a Tilt-a-Whirl. I hoped I wouldn't barf.

I congregated with the other southeastern whizzies around one of two podiums opposite of each other. A kid from Jackson compulsively cracked his knuckles, lacing his fingers and stretching them backwards, then grabbing his fingers to snap the joints. With each brittle pop my bones ached.

The announcer with plastic-looking hair and a permanent smile began to introduce members of the two teams. When he read off Hassan's name I saw his parents clap wildly. Of course we couldn't hear them through the soundproof walls. Patty flashed me a thumbs up.

Semi-finals worked the same way the district and regional matches except the contestants with the highest score would then square off for the finals. Those making the finals would be in the running for the $5,000 scholarship.

The time clock started ticking the second the reader began to fire toss-up questions. All around me buzzers were ringing and voices were shouting. I felt like I was standing in another room behind a wall of soundproof glass looking in. I glanced over at Patty. I couldn't stop thinking about the hug she'd given Hassan. I wondered what it might feel like to have her arms wrapped around me. I flubbed up one question and correctly answered another about the Civil War. Our team still managed to come out ahead at the end of the round. For round two the teams got to choose an area of expertise. The other side went first.

One of the guys on the northeastern team stood at an angle toward the camera. At the beginning of the competition he'd had a small dot of perspiration on the back of his pink shirt. Beneath the super-hot, bright lights it continued to grow, spreading in diameter. By the first round it was the size of a dinner plate. The other team successfully answered all five questions for the maximum amount of points. They were pulverizing us. Patty sat stiff and tense, as if at any moment she might snap, break in two.

Next it was our turn to choose.

Without checking with any of us, the kid from Jackson called out, "Literature!"

I saw Hassan wipe beads of sweat off his forehead. His eyebrows were one determined line.

The announcer read off a set of index cards. "Pip is a character in what book?"

"*Great Expectations*," we all answered at once.

"For ten points name the author of that book."

Again we shouted out together, "Charles Dickens." It was incredible. It was as if the questions came to us gift-wrapped.

"Correct. Dickens was born in the year—"

"1812," I called out. We needed one more answer in order to clinch the round. That one kid's shirt was completely drenched. We were tied with the other team.

"Correct. And finally, for twenty points, name the person actually responsible for giving Pip his allowance so that he could live the life of a gentleman."

Magwitch, of course. My finger hovered above the bell. Just like an ancient Persian carpet I found myself walking between borderlands, among rows of trees, down ravines, over fast-flowing creeks, winding and roaming. I could see the other side; it wasn't far.

Focus, I told myself.

Against a mossy background I heard Daddy calling my name. Daddy with all his peculiar ways. He was as much a mystery to me as I was to him. Daddy, a prisoner, hands reaching out to me.

Ding.

"Magwitch," Hassan answered.

Patty jumped up. I was afraid she might break out dancing. Hassan released a smile of surprise.

I was still going over in my head what had just happened. I knew the answer. I'd had it. I stared down at my empty hands. I'd given him that answer; it should have been mine.

The coach made a couple of quick changes and subbed in another player for me. I sat in a cramped corner of the room watching the third and final round. I couldn't explain it, but I had stopped caring. Deep down inside the only thing I wanted was to see my dad.

Before I knew it the bell sounded and the match was over. The southeastern team had won and Hassan, having scored the most points, would be going on to the finals. The announcer with lacquered hair handed me a play-at-home edition of the *Whiz Kidz* game. I joined Patty and the others in the next room.

There was a ten-minute break while they set up for Finals.

"I think you've been a good influence on my son," Mr. Reza said. He gazed at me through his oversized-frame glasses. "Hassan is much too interested in playing that silly game Pong on the television set."

I nodded.

The final match began. Hassan faced off against an eighth grader from Bexley, a rich suburb of Columbus. The Bexley kid wore braces and had a smug look on his face. Hassan matched him point for point as the score went back and forth. Patty sat next to me with her hands clenched in her lap.

The reader set up for a sudden-death bonus round to break the tie. "Name the capital of Rhodesia—"

The kid buzzed in first. His self-assuredness turned into confusion. "Wait! Is this a trick question? There is no more Rhodesia. It's Zimbabwe. Zimbabwe became a country in April."

The reader immediately recognized the question as being out of date and turned to the moderator. But before a judgment could be made, the player began to mock the judges.

"*What?* You guys are so stupid. You can't keep up with current events. *Hello!* Don't you guys ever read a newspaper? This is ridiculous. I mean, *geez*, come on. This is the state finals, for pity's sake." He bonked his head down on the table.

The moderator stood up. "I'm sorry, you will have to be removed for unsportsmanlike conduct. The rule book is clear—no head banging."

The coach of the other team appealed to the judges, who upheld the ruling. Suddenly it was all over.

Patty reached over and hugged me. It was over so quickly, the hug. I only wish it had lasted longer.

A photographer jumped in front of Hassan and snapped a picture of him being awarded a very large mock check for $5,000. We all swarmed into the tiny studio to congratulate him.

Mr. Reza squeezed into the tight-knit circle and pounded Hassan on the back. "This is a great day," he said. "Roland, please do us the honor of joining us for a celebratory dinner. We have reservations at a steakhouse. Patty you are welcome too."

It had been forever since I'd last tasted steak, or for that matter meat not out of a can. It would have been so easy to tag along and skip visiting Daddy. I certainly wasn't looking forward to being in a disinfectant-smelling hospital.

Patty checked with her parents and said it was all right for her to go with the Rezas.

As we exited the building, I reluctantly told them I'd meet them in a little bit. I had to see my dad before visiting hours were over. We arranged to meet up in the McDonald's parking lot of where we'd eaten earlier. "Bye." I waved to Patty and Hassan as they climbed into his parent's car.

I walked across the university campus to the hospital carrying my *Whiz Kidz* board game under my arm. I entered the lobby and scanned the directory. Visiting hours were from six to eight p.m. *All children under the age of sixteen must be attended by an adult.* Trying not to draw attention to the fact that I was underage *and* unaccompanied by an adult, I slipped into an open elevator and pressed a random number. I exited the elevator on the fourth floor right across from the nurses' station and approached a pretty nurse standing on the other side of the desk.

"Hi. I was visiting my grandpa with my folks and went to go get a snack from the machines downstairs and now I can't find my way. Can you tell me what floor and the room number for Harland Tanner?" I got back into the elevator and got off on the right floor.

The hallways smelled of Pine-Sol. My sneakers squeaked like styrofoam on the shiny-waxed linoleum floor. I walked slowly past the doors, reading the numbers until I found Daddy's room. I swallowed and stepped inside.

An oxygen tank hung over his bed as if it was standing guard. A spiderweb of tubes encircled him; some were attached to his veins and one was going into his nose. I was shocked at how much weight he'd lost—for already being so skinny. He was a slip of the old Daddy, tucked in between pillows and blankets, grizzled and gray against the clean white sheets. He opened his mouth and I noticed he didn't have his teeth in. "Hey, boy," he puffed out between dry, cracked lips.

I thought I said hey back, but might have only mumbled the words. I was still trying to get my bearings. Beside me was a blue screen with funny squiggles displayed on it. A beep-beep-beep kept time to Daddy's heartbeat. "How ya doing?" I asked.

"About as good as a dying man can, I reckon. Have a seat?" He took a shallow breath and quivered for a moment.

Trying not to bump any of the instruments or disturb any wires, I pulled a chair up to Daddy's bedside. It had a hole in the center for toileting a patient. I sat on it anyway.

"How's your Ma?"

"Fine." I wondered if I should let Daddy know the lights got turned back on. Perhaps he had no idea of the trouble we were going through. I decided to let the matter alone.

"How's your granny?"

"Oh, you know, the same."

"Yeah, she always was the meanest woman I'd ever met. Don't let that old windbag get to ya. Kick 'er one for me, will ya?"

"Sure, Daddy."

For a long second there was only the beeping sound and the wisp of oxygen as Daddy drew a ragged breath. There were a thousand and one things I had wanted to say, but they all seemed to pale. "Daddy," I began. He groaned. It looked like he was having trouble shifting his body. "Need some help there?"

"Don't mind if ya do."

I jumped up and refolded the pillows piled up underneath his scrawny frame. He was so light I could have lifted him with one hand. I sat back down. I knew if I tried to talk I would just end up blubbering, so I let Daddy do all the talking.

"Did I ever tell you that ya remind me of my brother, Leland?"

Daddy was never one for telling stories. I took his hand in mine.

"Well, ya do." He coughed and his whole body shook.

"Hush. No need to spend yourself."

"*Spend?*" he sputtered, finally catching his breath. "Spending is what I do best. Now, getting money is another thing entirely.

"Lee was the smartest feller I've ever met." Daddy went on. "He was always reading books. And, back then, books were hard to come by. Scarcer even than cash."

I guess I came by my reading naturally after all.

"He was just like you, with his head up in the clouds."

I didn't think that description fit me. Maybe Daddy's brother.

"Always telling folks they'd be seeing him later, after he came into his own. Making big plans, that boy, was."

195

Daddy went into coughing fit. I quick got him an ice chip from a pink plastic pitcher on the bedside stand. Little dribbles of water ran down his chin and pooled on his pillow. "Rest some," I urged.

"Me and Lee, we ran liquor for a few guys we'd met in town. Daddy been dead . . . well, for a while at least. Mama was half crippled from the polio. Drug her one leg behind her, she did. At the time the whole country was poor." He snorted and almost choked. "Being poor was nothin' new to us. We'd always been that a way. Hell, we was scrappin' metal before it became the patriotic thing to do. The rocky ground t'weren't good enough to grow seed and the woods had been overhunted. The only varmints around a boy might be able to catch were squirrels, raccoons, or a wild turkey."

Daddy's eyes glazed over. "You was always the smart one. So quick to have things figured out. It was all I could do, to stand back and watch you in pure amazement."

Maybe now was a good time to bring up the *Whiz Kidz* and how I'd made it to State, but before I could change the subject Daddy started up again.

"As soon as you heard about ol' man Roberts getting locked up for makin' liquor you decided we'd take over his business. You calculated we could make us enough money to make it through the winter. It was a risky thing to steal someone else's still, but you was a risk taker. Borrow it, you said, until ol' man Roberts needed it back."

The sickness must have clouded his brain. Daddy was confusing me with Lee. I gripped his hand tighter. "It's me, Daddy, Roland."

Daddy shook his head and his eyes cleared. "So we crept on back there one night. I remember the moon was full, and we were able to pick our way through the bramble bushes and thicket. Every little noise made me jump, but Lee, he just laughed."

The muted blue from the monitor cast an eerie glow over Daddy.

"We got a fire goin' and got the corn and hops abrewin' in the big old copper pot. I can still smell the sugar boilin'." Daddy had a smile on his weary-worn face, the kind you see on a sleeping baby. "We sat starin' into the flames and shootin' sparks, and Lee spoke out a poem he'd memorized by heart. Something about Gitche Gummy and the purple clouds of sunset."

Gitche Gumee? I thought.

"By God, Lee had a way about him."

Suddenly Daddy frowned and pulled his hand away from mine. He sat up and batted the space before his face. "Watch out there!"

I reached out and grabbed both of Daddy's hands. "Daddy, Daddy, it's okay. Settle, settle, please."

He collapsed back into his bank of pillows, silent for a while, before starting up again. I was getting a feeling by the way he was talking that Lee's story didn't come out good.

"We was ambushed by ol' man Robert's gang. Lee took off runnin' and got shot in the back."

I flinched.

"I was afraid to go home and tell Ma. And, oh my God." Tears streamed down Daddy's face.

"What, Dad? Does it hurt?"

"Yes, son, it does." Daddy sniffed a tear up inside his nose.

Daddy pounded his bed sheets with his fist. "I shoulda never let him get into such trouble."

I leaned forward. "Hush, Daddy, there weren't anything you could do." I tried to console him. "Hush, now." I smoothed back his thin straggly hair. He looked at me with his moist eyes and then closed them.

For a moment I thought he was almost asleep, but then he mumbled. "What, Dad?" I leaned closer to hear him, my ear only inches from his lips.

"Loved you."

"What?" I said, leaning ever closer.

A nurse in a starched white uniform entered the room. She took one look at Daddy in his weakened state and said to me, "You're going to have to leave."

"Loved you the best," he said so low that I wasn't sure I had heard right. With the little strength he had left Daddy squeezed my hand. "You, you're the one I'm proud of."

"Visiting hours are over," the nurse announced sternly.

I let go of Daddy's hand and tucked it underneath the blankets. His eyes were still closed. I hadn't told him about being in *Whiz Kidz* or my after-school job cutting grass.

Maybe next time.

I kissed Daddy on his stubbled cheek. He didn't seem to notice, except that a baby-sweet smile flickered across his face.

It was only later I realized I'd accidentally left the game by Daddy's bedside.

On the way home in the car, I nursed a headache that had come on in the hospital room and was now aggravated by the fact that I hadn't eaten since lunchtime. Rain pelted the windows. The windshield wipers scraped across the glass, making dreary smears of the red taillights in front of us. Up and down, back and forth, red, green, and yellow. Like a Persian carpet. Like the craziest of quilts.

I turned and pressed my face against the cool glass window. *Loved you the best.*

I pinched my nose to keep back tears. *You're the one I'm proud of.*

As I dozed off to the hypnotizing tick-tock of the windshield wipers, stories and words burrowed into my subconscious, into my heart. Once again, I saw the sorrow in my daddy's eyes as he spoke about Lee, and—*oh my God.*

Jesus or God, Allah or the Twelfth Iman. Pip's prisoner in the graveyard. Please help Daddy to get better.

Kinsman, Brother, Friend

I pulled my bike out of the rack in front of the school and shook half a dozen cicadas off the seat. They had begun to hatch earlier in the week, googly red-eyed insects the size of my index finger, emerging from underground near the roots of trees. They clung to whatever they could attach themselves to: mailbox posts, the carcass of the Datsun lying in the ravine, Granny's vinyl chair.

Soon after hatching they molted a tobacco-brown tissue-paper exoskeleton. I could barely walk without crunching and cracking them under my feet like dry leaves. Granny had taken to netting and frying them up in her black-iron skillet with a bit of grease. "Taste just like bacon," she stated, wings and legs sticking out between her gapped front teeth.

I eased out of the school driveway, trying to avoid rolling over cicadas. It was the last day of school.

At the very end of our last class Kyle came up to me. "There's a party at my house this afternoon. An end-of-the-school year thing."

Was this information or an invitation? "I've heard," I answered.

"So are you coming?"

Ever since the meet in Columbus, after seeing Daddy so bad off, I hadn't felt like doing much of anything. I think Mama understood; she never asked where I was going when I went out walking. I especially needed to be out of the house at sunset. I hated the feeling that came over me when all the light seeped out of the trailer. Granny kept saying for me to quit my moping. But Mama just told her to lay off.

I scuffed at the shiny school linoleum with my grass-stained sneakers. "I've got a job after school cutting grass," I told Kyle.

It wasn't exactly a fib. My posters had gotten some traction. Several old ladies had called to see if I was available. I'd show up and check the gas, clean the blades, and, come to find out I knew something about motors, fire up the customer's lawn mower. The yards set on a slope were the worst, as I had to struggle to push the lawnmower back and forth against gravity. But at least I was bringing in some money.

Patty joined Kyle as we stood at the back of the classroom. "Can't you do it tomorrow? The job, I mean," she asked.

"My Mom is ordering pizza," Kyle added.

He wrote his address down for me. I recognized it; it was a street where I'd done a lawn job the weekend before.

"If I can, I'll meet you there." I took the slip of paper from Kyle and then went back to double check that my desk was cleaned out.

I couldn't believe I had made it through a whole year. I couldn't believe Kyle had actually invited me to his pizza party. So much had happened since taking that placement test. There were times when I didn't know if being gifted was a gift or a curse. Of course if I had stayed at Stuart I'd have never met Hassan or Patty. I might have been a Whiz Kid, but never advanced as far as the Semi-Finals in Columbus. You need a team to get somewhere like that. I was reluctantly grateful for Kyle, even though we got off to a bad start. In the end he seemed like someone I could have been friends with. But now eighth grade was over.

Ms. Knudsen watched me as I stared into the well of my desk before closing the lid. "I never got a chance to tell you how much I enjoyed having you in my class." She came and stood next to me.

"Listen," she began, "the high school has a Pen & Quill Club. I know the faculty advisor. I hope you decide to join."

"Uh, thanks."

"When you first came I didn't know if you'd make it," she said.

That makes two of us, I thought.

"And, of course, when that thing happened between you and Kyle, I fought for you to stay."

I looked at her. Was I hearing right? *They were going to kick me out?*

She pointed to my head. "There's so much that goes on inside there. I wish I knew what you were thinking."

No she didn't. It was a jumble of loose ends. Sentence fragments. Fractions. Sometimes I didn't know what I was thinking.

"Well, you better get going. I hear there's a party at Kyle's. Have fun."

"Thank you, Ms. Knudsen." My voice sounded small and thin. "For everything."

As I neared Kyle's house I saw Hassan and Patty tear around a corner with Kyle close behind, chasing them with a double-barreled water gun. He pumped it and shot a torrent of water. I dropped my bike and used my backpack as a shield while Patty and Hassan crept up behind Kyle, each with colored water balloons.

Pow! Pow! Splat!

The balloons exploded over Kyle's shirt and head. I escaped to the back yard, where there were tubs of water balloons and other kids already pelting each other. Kyle was mostly holding his own against an army of us, windmilling water balloons as fast as he could offload them. I thought I was on Hassan's and Patty's team until I realized—there were no teams. Patty ran over and stuffed a water balloon inside my shirt. I got her back by doing the same, yanking her shirt and dropping one down the front. I think there was a goddess in our mythology unit saddled with many breasts. There was no time to be embarrassed, though later I would think about it over and over. I wrapped my arms around her from behind trying to squish the water out of the balloon, but only managed to squish the air out of her.

Patty and I stood looking at each other laughing until our laughter subsided into giggles. Meanwhile Hassan ganged up on us. It was every man, woman, and child for themselves. It was all-out war, a war to end all water balloon wars, the mother of all wars, survival of the fittest until the water balloons ran out.

When the battle ended, Patty and Hassan collapsed into a dripping heap in Kyle's back yard. I sprawled down next to them. In the twiggy bushes and flower beds around his house little latex pieces of balloons hung like colored confetti. "This place is trashed," Kyle remarked.

Hassan pulled at his shirt. The fabric emitted a fart noise. Patty dangled her bare feet in front of my face. She was wearing a pair of cutoffs that showed off her legs just beginning to tan. I grabbed her foot and began tickling it until she cried out for mercy. I rolled over closer to her. "So what's the deal?" I got up the courage to ask. "How come your second toe is bigger than your big toe?"

"It's fairly common," she said matter-of-factly. "It's called Morton's toe."

The sun beat down on us, tightening our wet skin as it dried. It was a moment when everything felt right.

"I've signed up for Explorer's camp through the university. We'll be studying hands-on biodiversity and the impact humans have on the environment." I listened, amazed at how beautiful Patty made taking water samples from the Hocking River sound. "What about you, Roland?"

"Football practice starts up in August. I'm pretty sure I'll make the freshman team," Kyle jumped in.

The grass beneath us was thick and high. I was no expert, but it needed a haircut. "I'll be working on my tan while mowing lawns," I said, taking off my sopping-wet T-shirt to soak up some rays.

All this time Hassan had been silent. "How about you?" I asked. "What are your plans for the summer?"

He bit his lower lip, hesitating. "We're moving."

"*What?*" I started up from my reclining position.

"*Moving!*" Patty bleated.

"My father got a teaching position at MIT. In Massachusetts. We're going to move in a couple of weeks." He delivered the news piecemeal, in little bits.

Whenever I thought about high school, which was all the time lately, I'd imagined Hassan there. At least, I thought, I'd have one friend to sit with at lunchtime.

"You're just now telling me?" I spurted.

"My parents told me last night," he explained in a rush of words.

I whipped an overlooked runt water balloon at a tree nearby. Thousands of cicadas shrieked. The noise couldn't drown out the angry voices inside my head. My one second of feeling good was over.

I lay back down and wrapped my damp shirt over my eyes and ears to muffle the outside world.

Was it that Hassan was leaving or that I was staying? Was it that things change or that they never change fast enough?

"Hey, everybody," I heard Kyle's mother call out. "Pizza's here."

After a few minutes I pulled my shirt off my face and looked over at the picnic table where Patty, Hassan, Kyle, and the others had gathered. They didn't care about me. I was trailer trash. I gathered my T-shirt and rounded the corner for my bike abandoned in front of the house.

"Hey! Where're you going?" Hassan ran after me. He caught up with me just as I reached my bike.

"I don't know." I couldn't explain it, but I felt like I didn't belong. I picked my bike up off the ground. Then I put it down again. "I'd love to leave. Move to a big city. Be someone other than who I am."

"I used to feel the same way. Until—" Hassan paused as if lost in memories. "I mean home in Iran wasn't perfect, but there people knew me, knew everything about me, called me by my nickname. My grandparents, aunts and uncles, they could tell a joke or story and we would all understand why it was funny. I miss playing football with my friends, hearing my language spoken. I even miss my cousins playing tricks on me."

"It's about being surrounded," I said. Then as an afterthought, "A cloud of witnesses."

His brow riddled, but a second later he laughed. "Thanks for everything, Roland. You've been great."

I didn't know what he was thanking me for. "Good luck in your new home."

Hassan nodded thoughtfully. "In Iran we have a tradition for saying good-bye." He stepped closer; a blade of grass stuck to his now dry skin. "We say, 'God keep you, God watch over you, God return you to us.'"

I wondered if his family in Iran had said these words, not knowing when Hassan left that it might be for good.

"You are my kinsman, you are my brother." He held out his hand for me to shake.

We couldn't do any of the things grownups do when they say goodbye—we couldn't promise to fly out and see each other or plan reunions. Even phone calls were expensive. I realized I'd probably never see him again.

I shook his hand. "Goodbye, my friend."

Riding back home, I stood up in the saddle in order to push up the last hill before steering breathlessly into the yard. Mama was out front watching two tawny-tinged hawks circle the sky overhead. One rose up on the current of the wind as the other swooped and dove. I laid down my bike and walked over to her and reached my arms around her, or around most of her. Up above, one of the hawks screamed.

Mama let out a sob. "He's gone, Roland."

The Ashes Are Spilt

Angie and Bill drove Mama and me up to Columbus to fetch Daddy's ashes. We'd decided to have him cremated because it was cheaper than a funeral. It didn't seem right to spend thousands of dollars we didn't have on Daddy now that he was dead. If he'd been alive he would have said so himself. No, we were better off doing things the quick and easy way. That's how he would have wanted it.

It surprised me how heavy the little box of ashes felt, but, taking into account it was a whole body, I guess it made sense. Still, Daddy had been so skinny—only flesh and bones. The weighty stuff—who he was, how he could take an engine apart and put it back together again, the twinkle in his eye whenever Mama came into the room, the anger that flared up in him and lit him on fire—that was all gone. The spirit—it ain't nothing but air, and the soul—who knows where it goes?

I've always wondered what happens when we die. Do we just rot in the ground, our remains becoming soil for the seed which grows? So that in a sense all that has gone before—pioneers and Indians, moonshiners and miners—are with us even now? The hills beneath my feet.

Or like in Granny's crazy stories, does our spirit roam? Wander like a frustrated haunt without a home, drift like a nomad over hills and deserts? Where does salvation lie—above or below the ground? In heaven or hell, or somewhere in between? In hope or in hoping, in the knowing or the unknown.

All we had left of Daddy was ashes.

When we got home that evening we sat around the kitchen table staring at the little metal casket.

Granny plodded into the kitchen, thumping her four-legged cane over the worn floor. "I hope you're not planning to keep 'im there. I don't think I could eat with him sitting right across from me like that. I know for sure I'd get indigestion—"

"Shut up, old woman," Mama expelled, like a sigh. I think we were all surprised. She held her head in her hands. "Let me think, will ya." Mama sounded more weary than angry. "He's been a-comin' and a-goin' as long as I've known him. So that now that we have him here, what we gonna do with him?" She looked across the table at me.

It's true. All his life he had been looking for something—better pay, a better job, the grass was always greener somewhere else. Perhaps, all that sand in his shoes was just Daddy searching for his brother.

I knew what would make Daddy the happiest. "Let him go, I reckon."

So we got up and went outside. The early summer twilight stretched across the top of the hills and extended into long, long shadows. In the bushes fireflies flitted.

It took a while, Bill holding onto Angie, Angie supporting Granny, me helping Mama, Mama carrying Daddy, as we made our way down the hill. Down in the ravine the shadows had gone flat and a smoky mist was beginning to creep up. We assembled along the mossy banks of the creek.

Mama cleared her throat. "Your daddy wasn't a religious man, but he was God-fearing. I know he'd like for us to say some words over him."

Granny pulled in her lower lip like it was a dresser drawer. For once she had nothing to say.

Mama turned to Angie. "Angie-baby, you want to say goodbye to your daddy?"

Her face, usually fierce and sullen, now melted. I tried to remember the last time I'd seen Angie cry, really cry, not whine or pout or complain. The corners of her mouth turned down and when she spoke her voice cracked as if something was blocking her windpipe. "I love you, Dad—" was all she said before sinking to her knees, weeping hard and heavy tears. Bill got down on his knees too.

Crickets chirped in the darkness around us. There was no way to know. *The substance of things hoped for, the evidence of things not seen* that Gertie Haywood talked about.

I took the notebook Ms. Knudsen had given me out of my back jeans pocket. The penciled lines ran together as I read the words. "Daddy, I wrote this poem for you:

The Arrowhead

From the soft black earth came sharpened flint.
The point pierces, cutting core-deep
Slicing through bone and blood,
Into the marrow of the soul,
Back to the beginning.
Flesh of your flesh,
Seed of the father,
We walk the path
You and me,
Together.

All was silent until Granny finally broke the woeful spell cast upon us. "If'n that's a poem, how come it don't rhyme?"

"Leave off," Angie growled. "That's a beautiful poem, Roland."

Mama nodded her head in agreement. "It's amazin' how you do it, boy. Put all them words together to make a feelin'."

Granny sewed her lips up again.

I glanced around at each face. "What do we do now?"

Mama opened the oblong box. The breeze stirred the gray and silver ash. "Harland Tanner," she said, "you're free," and shook the contents into the creek. It swirled on top of the water like dirty foam before sinking to the silty bottom. In the treetops the cicadas offered a chorus and the night birds sang a hymn or two.

By morning Daddy would be long gone, down the Hocking to the Ohio, which meets the Mississippi, which flows into the Gulf of Mexico.

The next morning when I woke up the sun beat in through the window. I got up and looked through the screen door. Everything was where it was supposed to be, the tractor tire flower beds were still there in the front yard as well as a scattering of old junk. Yet— everything was all wrong. Daddy was dead, the world was broken like a china plate, and there was nothing I could do to mend it.

I took my breakfast, a biscuit with butter and jelly wrapped up in a napkin, and hiked down to the pine grove. There I sat beneath the swaying fir branches and tried to forget. Emptiness and loneliness were everywhere, inside and outside of me. I covered my eyes with my arm and cried.

There came a voice in the forest calling my name. Patty? I quick wiped my eyes.

She broke into the clearing. "Whew." She flopped down beside me. "You're a hard one to find."

"How did you—"

"Hassan drew me a map."

"He told you I might be here?"

"The movers are at his house. Or he would have come."

I nodded. "I know. He called me and we talked on the phone."

She surveyed the woods around us. "I heard." Was all she said. There was a solemn church-like note to her voice. "I'm sorry, Roland."

"S'kay."

She looked me in the eyes. "I get the feeling that I'm talking to you through a door. I'm trying to get the door open, but you're holding it from the other side."

"Sorry." Maybe I was like those seventeen-year cicadas cocooned underground. There must be some inner alarm clock telling them: *Now is the Time.*

I lay back onto the downy pine needles and gazed upward at the sky, at the clouds lazily floating by. They reminded me of the paper decorations Patty liked to hang up. "I see a horse," I said.

Patty lay next to me. "I see an amoeba, splitting."

It figures, I thought. "That fat one is where the horse sleeps."

"And then the cell gobbles up another one like a hungry PacMan, and, eww, it vomited."

"The horse just threw a shoe. See it there, it just broke off."

"I see a boy wandering lonely."

I thought a second. "I see him too. But, give it time, he'll meet up with them others." The cloud did its cloud-amoeba thing. "Look, lonely no more."

I was not Pip or a character in a book. This was my story, and I was writing it now, and always.

I took her hand, studied the webbing between her fingers and the lovely way her knuckles puckered. We stayed that way for a while, holding hands and watching the clouds grow and part across the chariot of sky.

Finally she said, "I have to go."

Of course, I thought. "I'll show you the way back out to the blacktop." I still had ahold of her hand.

We wound our way around thorns and thistles that weren't there in the spring when Hassan last came to visit. We paused by the side of the road where she'd stashed her bike in tall grass.

"I'll be around all summer," she said.

"So will I." I was staring into her eyes, dark blue pools, deep enough to swim around in.

"So," she began, "maybe we could hang out."

I cracked open the door. "I'd like that."

Suddenly, before I knew it, Patty was hugging me. Not a sympathy hug or one just to be nice. It wasn't like saying interesting. Her arms around my neck and her nose buried into my shoulder was a quickening. Perhaps like the Holy Ghost descending, like falling under the spell of something great and powerful and awesome.

I hooked my arms around her waist. She was so small I could almost wrap around her twice. We held each other close and for so long that time seemed to stand still. We stayed like that, tangled up.

"Don't you see," she whispered into my ear. "It's you I like."

I wasn't sure I'd heard her right. Maybe a cicada had plugged my ear. Even so, I pressed her to my chest harder. I climbed every last rung in the ladder of her spine.

Her lips migrated from my shoulder to my cheek and together my lips found hers. It was like pressing the buzzer at *Whiz Kidz*, a jolt of electric adrenaline shot through me. I felt if I didn't let go I might explode. Reluctantly I released her.

"When will I see you again?"

"I'll be in town almost every day mowing lawns. We can meet up at the Milk Shake Shack," I answered, still keeping a finger on her belt loop.

I glimpsed her picket-fence teeth as she breathed in through her mouth. "Sounds like a plan."

As she rode away, up and down the hills, I watched

the top of her head appear and then disappear from view. "Thank you," I breathed into the dust-hued horizon.

"Where you been?" Granny attacked as soon as I entered the trailer.

Mama must've seen something in my eyes. "Leave off, Granny. He's been out a-pondering, I can tell." She went into the bathroom to run me a shower.

When I came out of the bathroom I found that Angie and Bill had come over. They were all around the kitchen table playing cards. "Feel better, baby?" Mama asked, and Angie rolled her eyes at me while Granny sneaked a peek at Bill's hand.

"Yeah, thanks for asking," I said, curling up on the worn couch and pulling my blue- and white-striped notebook out of my book bag. It was almost full, nearly every page written on.

We are surrounded, therefore, by a great cloud of witnesses, I read.

The rise and fall of voices drifted over to me as Angie and Granny bickered with one another about who last played what card. My kin—surprises and contradictions every one of them.

Loud laughter burst forth from the kitchen, followed by hoots and cursing.

I smiled to myself. I am surrounded.

Acknowledgements

This book was a long time coming. It has been an exercise in perseverance in the face of self-doubt. I owe a lot of people a debt.

Thank you most of all to Nancy Sayre, my editor, who said the words "I love this manuscript," which set me on the road to publication. Your editorial and emotional support has surpassed all my expectations. Indeed, *great expectations!*

Love and gratitude to my critique group and first readers: Kurt Hoeksema, Curt Mortimer, Sarah Sullivan, Tammy Perlmutter, Tim Brandhorst, Claudia Guadalupe Martínez (check out her books!), Mary Jo Guglielmo, who coaxed me into starting a blog. *Cloud of Witnesses* was accepted into Highlights Foundation whole-novel workshop where the wonderful author Greg Leitich Smith helped me find a way in. Also thanks to Blueberry View Artist Retreat (Jan, Mark, and Bosco!) where I was able to spend a week revising the manuscript. Crystal Chan supplied candles, yoga mats, and a quiet place for my mind to wander both in grief and exaltation.

A big thanks to my family, Mike and Grace, for giving me the time and space needed to flourish as a writer. And to my community at large for accepting this crazy writer into your midst—you have given me so much, not the least being the freedom to create.

Credits

We give grateful acknowledgement to the following publications, in which excerpts from *Cloud of Witnesses* have appeared in a slightly different form:

"The Arrowhead," *Flash – An Anthology: flash fiction from authors touched by Kentucky*, edited by Ashley Parker Owen, 2012.

"It Came Upon a Midnight Clear," *Offbeat Christmas Story*, edited by Ashley Parker Owen, 2013.

"Cloud of Witnesses," *Hunger Mountain*, Spring 2010.

The author's translation of *Shahnameh* in Chapter 16 is based on the translation found in *Early Persian Poetry: From the Beginning Down to the Time of Firdausi*. Translated by A.V. Williams Jackson. 1920; The Macmillan Company, New York; pages 100-101.

About the Author

Jane Hertenstein is a prolific author of fiction and creative non-fiction for adults and children. She enjoys long-distance bike touring, waking up early to work, running along the lakefront, and working with the homeless on the streets of Chicago. Her latest book, *Cloud of Witnesses*, is based on her experiences substitute teaching in the foothills of the Appalachian Mountains in southern Ohio.

Janes loves to hear from her readers. You can contact her at:

jane.hertenstein@goldenalleypress.com
facebook.com/JaneHertensteinAuthor

CPSIA information can be obtained
at www.ICGtesting.com
Printed in the USA
LVHW091602270219
608932LV00002B/495/P

3/19